ADAM
IN EDEN

ADAM IN EDEN

CARLOS FUENTES

TRANSLATED BY
E. SHASKAN BUMAS AND
ALEJANDRO BRANGER

DALKEY ARCHIVE PRESS
CHAMPAIGN / LONDON / DUBLIN

Originally published in Spanish as *Adán en Edén* by Alfaguara, Mexico City, 2009
Copyright © 2009 by Carlos Fuentes
Translation copyright © 2012 by E. Shaskan Bumas and Alejandro Branger
First edition, 2012
All rights reserved

Fuentes, Carlos.
  [Adán en Edén. English]
  Adam in Eden / Carlos Fuentes ; translated by E. Shaskan Bumas and Alejandro
Branger. -- 1st ed.
     p. cm.
  "Originally published in Spanish as Adán en Edén by Alfaguara, Mexico City, 2009"
--T.p. verso.
  ISBN 978-1-56478-796-5 (cloth : alk. paper)
  I. Bumas, E. Shaskan, 1961- II. Branger, Alejandro. III. Title.
  PQ7297.F793A2 2012
  863'.64--dc23
                              2012033270

Partially funded by a grant from the Illinois Arts Council, a state agency.

La presente traducción fue realizada con el estimulo del Programa de Apoyo a la
Traducción de Obras Mexicanas a Lenguas Extranjeras (Protrad), dependiente de las
instituciones culturales de México convocantes.

This translation was carried out with the support of the Program to Support the
Translation of Mexican Works into Foreign Languages (ProTrad), with the collective
support of Mexico's cultural institutions.

www.dalkeyarchive.com

Cover: design by Mikhail Iliatov

Printed on permanent/durable acid-free paper and bound in the United States of America

Did I request thee, Maker, from my clay
To mould me Man? did I solicit thee
From darkness to promote me, or here place
In this delicious garden?

— Milton, *Paradise Lost*

1

I don't understand what happened. Last Christmas everybody was smiling at me, giving me gifts, congratulating me, predicting a new year—yet another year—of success, satisfaction, and just rewards. People nodded approval at my wife as though to tell her she was very lucky to be married to the toast of the town . . . Today I ask myself, what does it mean to be "the toast of the town . . . ?" Or, for that matter, burnt toast? I feel more *burnt* than *toasted*. Was this the year when my memory, so subject to illusions, at last grew disillusioned? Did what happened really happen? I don't really want to know. All I want is to go back to last year's Christmas: a family affair, comforting in its stark simplicity (in its inherent stupidity) and annual reoccurrence; a prophecy of twelve months to come that would not be as gratifying as Christmas Eve because fortunately they would not be as silly and wretched as Christmas; the holiday that we celebrate in December—just because—as a matter of course—without knowing why—out of custom—because we are Christians—we are Mexicans—war—war against Lucifer—because in Mexico we're Catholics to a man, not excepting the atheists— because a thousand years of iconography instructs us to kneel before the Nativity scene of Bethlehem even as we turn our backs on the Vatican. Christmas takes us back to the humble origins of faith. There was a time, another time, when to be Christian was to be called an atheist, to be persecuted, to hide, to flee. Heresy: a heroic path. Now, in our sorry age, to be an atheist shocks no one. Nothing is shocking. Nobody is shocked. What if I, Adam Gorozpe, were suddenly to knock down the little Christmas tree with my fist, smash the star, wrap a wreath around my wife Priscila Holguín's head as a crown, and—as they used to say—*to drum out* (whatever that means) my guests . . . ?

Why don't I do that? Why do I keep acting with my famous bonhomie? Why do I keep behaving like the perfect host who, every Christmas, invites friends and colleagues over, plies them with food and drink, gives each of them a different present—never the same tie twice, or the same scarf—even as my wife insists that 'tis the season for re-gifting the useless, ugly, or duplicate presents that were foisted on us, and for dumping them on those who, in turn, give them to other dupes who thrust them upon . . .

I look at the small mountain of gifts piled before the tree. I am overcome by the fear of giving a colleague the gift he gave me two, three, four Christmases ago . . . But thinking about this is enough to ward off my fears. My story isn't up to New Year's yet. It's still Christmas Eve. My family surrounds me. My innocent wife smiles her most conceited smile. The maids pass around punch. My father-in-law distributes cake and cookies from a tray.

I should not get ahead of myself. Today everything is fine; nothing awful has happened yet.

I look out the window distractedly.

A comet trails across the sky.

And my wife, Priscila, loudly slaps the maid who serves the cocktails.

2

Again a comet shoots across the sky. I am paralyzed with doubt. Is the bright heavenly body preceded by its own light or does it merely introduce the light? Does the light mark the beginning or the end? Does it presage birth or death? I believe the sun, the greater celestial object, determines whether the comet is a *before* or *after*. In other words: the sun is the master of the game; the comets are specks, chorus members, the extras of the universe. And yet, we are so accustomed to the sun that we only notice its absence, its eclipse. We think about the sun when we do not see the sun. Comets, though, are like launched rays of solid sunlight, emissary beings, ancillaries to the sun, and in spite of everything, proof of the existence of the sun: without servants, there is no master. A master needs servants to prove his own existence. I ought to know. As I am a modern lawyer and businessman who can vouch for my whereabouts five times a week (Saturday and Sunday being holidays), taking my place at the head of the conference table, my subordinated subordinates spaced before me, even if I behave like a modern boss, in a non-arbitrary way, I am like a sun that wants to give warmth but not to burn. And in spite of everything, is it not true that I am the boss only because they agree I am? Do the comets make us think about the sun? Do the former give meaning to the latter? I don't know if every man in my position thinks about these things.

I rather doubt it. A powerful man takes his power for granted, as if he'd been born not naked but swaddled in richest fabrics, with not just a silver spoon in his mouth, but a golden crown upon his head. I look at my employees seated around the table, and I would like to ask them if I am their sun, or nobody's son? Am I powerful on my own or because you, who could get a job anywhere, give me power? Would I lack power without you? Who is more powerful: you who give me power, or I who exercise it?

Today's comet is only a comet because it is visible with the naked eye. How many celestial bodies circulate the heavens every day without our knowledge? Are we all bearded astrological bodies, preceded by light, or caudate bodies, succeeded by luminosity? Let's say I was a comet, then what would my tail be like? Diffuse: branching out in different directions? Or horn-shaped: a corporate chairman with a curved tail? Unexpected or scheduled: a heavenly body, unique and unimaginable, until it appears, or a predictable and therefore boring comet, which is to say, not a lot of comet?

Time—for our purposes, this narrative—will tell.

Are Saturdays and Sundays really *holidays*? And is a holiday a day of rest, or just a busy shopping day?

I won't say—or hope not to say—but presiding over the Board of Directors today, I allow myself the perk—willful, determined—of draping my leg over the chair's armrest and swinging it absently. Let's see who else dares?

And dare I explain to myself why I am successful?

3

Why did I marry her? While you try to picture me, picture yourselves as me. My career was just beginning. I was a law intern. I hadn't even submitted my thesis to receive the degree. I was, by most definitions, a nobody.

She, however . . .

I saw her picture in the newspaper every day. She was the Queen of Spring, driven on La Reforma Avenue in an allegorical car (to the indifference of pedestrians, true). She was the Princess of the Mazatlán Carnival (and later princess of the one in Veracruz). She was Godmother of the Tezozómoc Brewery and of its philanthropic subsidiary benefiting nursing homes. She grandly opened stores, movie theaters, highways, spas, churches, cantinas . . . and these honors did not come to her because she was the prettiest young woman around.

Priscila Holguín was what people call attractive. Her round little face was redeemed by the sparkle of her innocent eyes, the cleanliness of her Colgate smile, the dimples on her cheeks, her Shirley Temple curls, and a nose so minuscule as to not require surgical intervention. She was the kind of woman referred to as a cutie-pie. She was neither a great beauty in the national molds of María Felix or Dolores del Río, nor was she ugly like so many squat, dark-skinned, overweight, redundant, earnestly good or perversely bad women lacking the great and rare perfection of those movie-star *mestizas* but destined to become brides (when young) and, with luck, tolerable matriarchs (when old). Gray hair makes everyone look distinguished.

Priscila Holguín represented the golden mean. She was anything but ugly. She was even a little beautiful. She was what is known as a pleasant-looking woman. Her looks neither offended ugly women nor brought unwanted competition to beauties. That made her the perfect girlfriend. She was a threat to no one. And this absence of danger made her more enticing than the man-eaters or the not-so-hot tamales.

Her talent was that she not only reigned over useless ceremonies, but that, as though she suspected the pointlessness of her monarchy, she adorned those ceremonies with snatches of songs. And so, after being crowned Queen of This or Princess of That, she would conclude the ceremony by singing, *"Keep lying to me, because your wickedness makes me happy"* or *"out on the big ranch, out where I used to live"* or *"there are no doormen or neighbors"* or *"on the bank of the blue lagoon of Ipacaraí."*

The songs were not requirements listed in the job description for queen or princess, but everybody expected Priscila's signature flourish, as if that closing ditty was proof that her right to reign was not based solely on her beauty (which was slight) but was instead a prize for her talent (at singing pop songs). Or maybe the other way around: Priscila was first and foremost a singer, and her crown was incidental, a kind of trophy she received in recognition of her achievement in the art of singing. Or to return to the first way around: the ditty would make up for her lack of traffic-stopping beauty, allowing a plain Jane to attract attention.

No wonder—I would read, I would laugh—Priscila was courted by the richest kids in town, the heirs apparent of the captains of industry: the pretty-faced boys, the Maserati drivers, the smooth talkers. Wasn't Priscila a constant passenger of convertible sports cars and Acapulco yachts, a regular in ringside seats at the bull-fights? Was she not inaccessible, except through the medium of the *Club Reforma* social pages? How might someone without access to the proper channels arrange an audience?

One day she was advertised as the Godmother of the Auto Show. All the big European and Japanese carmakers were on display (not the Americans, whose past glories were segregated in a museum-like display, and whose clunky late models were relegated to the category of all-terrain vehicles): Mercedes Benz, Audi, Alfa Romeo, Citroën, BMW, Lexus. I entered the exhibition space, blinded by the glaring profusion of dazzling metals, luxuriously designed bod-ies, expectant headlights, and tires of shiny black polished rubber, vaguely doubting that these flashy cars could drive around with impunity through Mexico City without being exposed to potholes, ridicule, the scrape of a key, maybe a car-jacking, vengeful destruc-tion following the cry of resentment for the power projected onto that object: why you but not me, dickhead?

I knew then that I had to mask any sign of the resentment I shared with the many have-nots toward the few haves-lots.

Can a luxury car incite a revolution? Let them eat cake? Let them drive a Maserati? I had no desire to put my suspicions to the test. Instead, walking through the exhibition that would be reigned over by the Empress of the Steering Wheel (AKA Priscila Holguín), I repeated to myself the saying: "Smooth talker trumps pretty face, and Maserati trumps smooth talker."

Priscila's Pretty-faced Maserati-driving Smooth talkers (P.M.S.) surrounded her to make sure that she would be everybody's or nobody's. I suddenly grasped the situation. The court of suitors surrounded her not because of who she was but because of what she represented; she could endorse a brand because she herself was also a brand: Priscila-approved Maserati or Priscila's Corn-Flakes or Coca-Cola as drunk by Priscila. To approach her was to be beside not a luminous being, but a familiar status symbol. The pretty-faced, Maserati-driving, smooth-talking boys wanted to show her off, not to win her heart. Whomever she chose to go out with got the prize, was photographed with the Queen, Princess, and Godmother; he would never see her again, because once was enough for him to have obtained the endorsement testified to by having gone out with Priscila, and Priscila never went out twice with the same young man, lest her public imagine that the display was genuine, that she was his girlfriend or wife: nuh-uh, no way baby. I saw her, I understood her. Priscila had to be young, single, available, but never anybody's partner, because being somebody's partner meant excluding all her other suitors, leaving each of them without the hope of becoming anything more than a P.M.S., without the hope of becoming a new suitor, boyfriend, husband, and thus the one who would sacrifice all the other young men, *mirabile dictum*, preventing them from obtaining the reward that eligible bachelors would get for having gone out, having been seen, with the Queen of And-So-On. Therefore—as I imagined correctly—in the end Priscila Holguín was the bait that gave an aura of irresistible attraction to whomever went out with her, preparing him to choose, with infinite patronizing and a trace of disdain, the young woman who would become his life partner, the mother of his children, the Pyrrhic victor over the Princess of Princesses.

At the center of the Auto Show, I saw Priscila just as she was: an invention of marketing, a young woman who did not endanger the prospective girlfriend or wife of the eligible bachelors who besieged her around a vintage Cadillac. I slipped past my competitors—as I considered them at the moment. I reached Priscila, took her by the hand, and said:

"Let's blow this pop stand. I'll buy you a coffee at Sanborns."

4

As always, I assembled my colleagues for a meeting on the day after the Feast of the Three Kings. Today, few countries celebrate the Epiphany, the arrival in Bethlehem of the Magi Gaspar, Melchior, and Balthasar bearing gifts for the newborn baby Jesus. I suppose that in Mexico we commemorate the Magi to celebrate the end of our only real holiday season, which begins with *las posadas*, the nine days before Christmas, and continues into the New Year until Three Kings Day. Then we scatter little holidays here and there such as the Feast of The Presentation of the Lord in February, Benito Juárez's birthday and the anniversary of the expropriation of oil in March, more of the same in April, Mother's Day in May. We take comfort in the fact that the only reason Spaniards have more saints, and therefore more holidays, than we Mexicans do is that they had a head start on us. We're playing catch-up. That's only difficult because we don't invoke such Aztec gods as, say, Saint Huichilobos.

While getting all spiffed up and thinking about the holiday, I'm getting off subject. I, your humble narrator, have little to celebrate this January 6, when I walk into the boardroom to deal with matters of the utmost urgency with my business associates: I know them extremely well; I do not hire strangers; I want my entire team to be trustworthy and not just, as the tongues wag, inferior to the boss, to me, as though a superior man—or woman—could, somehow, even slightly diminish the image that I have of myself, an image that is no way presumptuous. My career proves that I've achieved all I have through my own efforts, which now gives me the right to choose whomever I please to work with.

The gossip is that my associates are deferential and meek. The gossips say that I won't admit anyone smarter than I am into my inner circle. That type of accusation has only been made by those left outside of what one columnist has called "the magic circle that surrounds Adam Gorozpe." I knew there was a reason I kept that columnist on my payroll.

All right then. Today I walk into the boardroom, glancing at my watch, hurrying and relaxed at once (another secret of my success), without looking at anyone in particular. Some assistant I can't see pulls out my chair for me. I sit. I fix my eyes on the files. I review the documents, deriving pleasure from confirming that they are all blank, and that the world is deceiving itself! I remove my glasses and wipe them with a Kleenex from a box on my left (thinking sarcastically that the little snots are on the left). I put on my glasses, and I finally look up to give my attention to the eleven consultants—not twelve, because that would make me number thirteen, and saviors tend to wind up crucified, I say to myself on this day when I resume work rested, alert, tanned by the Caribbean sun, no longer on vacation.

My eleven associates are wearing dark sunglasses.

They are not looking at me.

Or they are looking at me in darkness.

Eleven pairs of sunglasses.

"No need to exaggerate," I joke. "It was pretty cloudy in Cancún."

My joke is met with silence.
Twenty-two dark lenses stare at me.
Without mercy.
What happened?

5

When things turn out badly for me, as happened today, January 6, I take refuge in reflections on my father-in-law, Don Celestino Holguín, remembered (and forgotten) as the King of Bakery and father of my wife, the Queen of Spring (as I already explained). The Bakery and the Spring are kept apart from each other by the same device that kept the cruel winter from the Virgin of Guadalupe: a miracle.

From the moment we were introduced, I've been amazed that Don Celestino built his fortune on a pile of sweet breads. They say that man does not live by bread alone, but my father-in-law had disproved this saying: he had lived very well by bread, and bequeathed his bread rolls to his children and then to me, his soon-to-be son-in-law. Don Celes turned the curse with which God cast Adam and Eve out of Paradise—"You shall earn your bread by the sweat of your brow"—into a blessing, even more so in a country like Mexico that takes great pride in the variety and deliciousness of its breads, in tough competition with France and Central Europe, where nevertheless no bakery produces such beautiful and varied goods as our dinner rolls and sandwich rolls, our poetically named frogs, ears, sugar-freckled buns, conch-shells, brides, as well as our mixed-layer puff pastries and the powdery shortbreads that are sweetened, stick-like, monochrome glazed pastries . . . We live a paradox in our poor country with its rich cuisine. Beginning with breakfast: huevos rancheros and divorced eggs (legally separated by two salsas), tamales and bean casserole, chilaquiles and enchiladas, quesadillas and sopes, preceded by papayas and oranges, sapodillas (or black sapote), mamey sapotes (on a pink-to-orange spectrum), water- and other melons, bananas (jamaica, silk, horn plantain, and sucrier), soursops (white with black seeds), and prickly pears (green as envy).

Sometimes I wonder if Mexico is a poor country because it wastes so much time preparing sumptuous meals, followed by long hours savoring them.

"Look at the gringos," I indoctrinate the ingrates of my Board when they ask me for permission to take a two-hour lunch. "The gringos eat at noon standing on their feet like horses, quick, then get on with their work . . ." I pause for effect. "And they eat dinner at six in the evening: lettuce with strawberry jam, dry chicken, and for dessert Technicolor Jell-O."

"Would you like us to bring our lunches to the office, sir?" asks a smart ass.

I smile with leniency:

"No, my friend. Have a hearty breakfast of beans and empanadas to keep your stomach from growling."

They all laugh.

Or, rather, they all used to laugh.

My father-in-law was one of a kind. His vocation of baker seemed to have given him a sense of fulfillment larger than a wedding cake. Don Celes's work was sanctioned by the biblical command—"you shall eat your bread," and so on—which for him was more blessing than reproach.

"I bet you that Jehovah didn't say," Don Celes offered, "you shall eat your steaks or you shall eat your omelet or you shall eat your salpicón or you shall sip your broth by the—"

"Sweat of your face?" I said, anticipating his biblical exegesis.

"Exactly," Don Celes agreed, approving of my lucidity and all but congratulating himself that his little girl, Priscila, had chosen a husband as great as me, to whom Don Celes could delegate the running of the business and who could shepherd the transition from baking to more lucrative, if less necessary, activities.

"They call you Adam. Adam, after all, is your name," my father-in-law elaborated. "So you have the same name as the first man who, instead of loafing around Eden, had to labor for his daily bread, *to earn his bread*—does everybody understand me?—by the sweat of his face."

And turning to his daughter:

"You chose your husband well, Priscila. Who would have thought that this penniless bum you married would become a thousand times wealthier than his father-in-law, me, and by the sweat of his face alone?"

"Now, Daddy, you know that bread doesn't sweat," Priscila answered before taking a glass of watermelon juice from the maid, whom she thanked with a slap across the face.

But Don Celes had already turned his attention to the other person at the table, his son Abelardo.

"Come on, Abelardo, can't you be more like your brother-in-law? Why not emulate him just a *little*, huh?"

The young man to whom Don Celes spoke was an unusual person for whom, though he was still a boy when we first met, I had immediately felt respect. In all sincerity, I have to admit that nobody else in the Holguín family, neither my wife, her father, nor her deceased mother, God rest her soul, inspired more respect in me than this quiet boy, impervious to his dad's verbal pressure and to his sister's eminent silliness. Such is the situation even in the best families. There's always an exceptional being about whom one asks oneself, where did this person come from? Obviously not from his father or his sister or his deceased Mamacita And-So-On whose bedroom and bathroom were preserved as a kind of shrine to tackiness; because And-So-On so loved pink, everything in her room—curtains, walls, bed, pillows, rugs, comforters, chairs—was that color, and there was even a rose-tinted mirror, as if to give Doña Rosenda back her self-esteem (though I can't imagine she ever lost it). One detail alone—a white camellia in a vase—clashed with the bedroom's symphony in pink. There was also an iron bidet, solid enough to resist any and all onslaughts.

"She was romantic," Don Celes had said, without any further explanation, dogma for his loyal servant, obviously me, concerning the virtues of the household to which I had the honor of being admitted.

The bathroom's pinkness also included pink toilet paper, and—as I discovered when I pulled a pink chain—pink water. Everything was pink, save that iron bidet and the camellia. And save Doña Rosenda herself who, in preparation for death, had prematurely dyed her hair a natural blonde.

Convinced that the Holguín family practiced a kind of dull and conventional eccentricity, I paid attention to the young Abelardo because he was neither dull nor eccentric, except within the norm of his family. Tall, thin, silent, he seemed to belong to a different species. He was no Holguín.

"Was he adopted?" I asked Priscila one day, in a mocking tone.

"Don't be rude!" she rebuked me. "You foul-mouthed bastard! *Two little trees have grown on my ranch!*"

I tried in vain to discern a logical relation between my question and these arboreal insults. That was Priscila. For her no cause led to any effect. Under no circumstances. That is why we did not have any children.

"I love your little tummy," I told her with much affection. "I want to make it bigger and bigger."

"Until I'm pot-bellied?" she said, infuriated. "You'd rather I had a pot-belly? Is that what you want, you monster? To see me deformed? Are you that apathetic?"

"Actually that wouldn't count as a deformity."

"Oh really? What else do you call ruining my figure? You know who gave me my figure? The Lord God gave it to me, and only He can take it away . . ."

"On the day you die," I said without meaning for it to come out the way it did.

"Oh! So that's what you want! To kill me! Spineless creep!"

"That's not what I said . . ."

"To fatten me up like a carnival balloon until I explode, you coward, fool, ass-kisser! *Out on the big ranch!*"

As I said, Priscila's outbursts were usually delivered out of conversational context.

No, she did not refuse me her "favors." But she guarded them with so many precautions that in the end I would lose not just my passion, but also my pleasure. Fortunately, everything took place in the dark. Priscila never saw my genitals. Better off that way! I never saw hers. The worse for me!

"Turn off the light."

"Okay, fine."

"Don't look at me."

"How could I possibly see you? It's too dark."

"Touch me with mercy."

"What's that supposed to mean?"

"Touch my scapulars."

"You don't have any scapulars."

"Dummy."

"Oh."

The problem was that she *did* wear scapulars where she should *not* have, so my moves felt sacrilegious. How was I to caress the Sacred Heart of Jesus? How was I to suck on the breasts (and whatever else) of Our Lord of Sorrows? How to penetrate, in short, the Holy of Holies covered by the Veil of Veronica? This last one was a temptation of a subtlety scarcely attributable to Priscila, who was perhaps unaware of Veronica's questionable past, because she confused her with Mary Magdalene; she believed they were both sisters of the Lord, reformed by religion, and therefore stripped the Virgin Mary of her virginity, unless the girls were younger than Jesus, in which case, as they say in roulette, *rien ne va plus*, and everyone to Bethlehem!

"The wildest Negro I met in Havana," Priscila sang when I had satisfied her.

All this took place in the dark. So she never saw me naked. Better still.

6

Whoever reads this will understand that he who writes it needed a safe haven outside of his home. To forget about the Holguín family. Their living and their dead. To be able to look at myself in the mirror without blushing, because Priscila and her family embarrassed me and made me ashamed of them and of myself.

I gave the Holguíns just as much as or more than they gave me to reassert my authority (still shaky because I'd hit the jackpot by marrying Priscila, which allowed me to bound up the social ladder from the crowded rungs of nobodies to the spacious heights of somebodies, beyond what my merits entitled me to, if not below my own weaknesses). The Holguíns gave me the gift of contrast: by being both what I was and what I am with them, I had the enormous freedom to be *someone else* when I left the house to pursue my career.

My detractors say that Don Celestino bankrolled me. I suppose that's so, but I turned out to be a very good investment. I paid back his loan with exorbitant interest. I drew a line. In the house of Lomas Virreyes, I would adapt to the eccentricities of the family. Outside of it, I would be my own man. Free from the influence of those at home. Do not transfer any phone calls to me, Ms. Secretary, from my wife or father-in-law. Fulfill their requests yourself, as long as they are important (money, property, and unavoidable meetings). Ignore the nonsensical requests (hair-salon schedules, complaints about the help, dinner plans with people who aren't important, I've got a major headache, Why don't you love me the way you used to?, Where did you put the car keys?, Can I hang a picture of the Pope in the living room?).

My office is my sanctuary, inviolable by definition, sacred by vocation. My private life is denied entrance. Because my employees know this, they treat me with the respect that a man—such as I am—about whom they *know nothing* outside of work, deserves. My office, unlike most, is an image of privacy. My house is an agora of hullabaloo, silliness, gossip, and blackmail by those who think they've got you by the nuts just because they knew you when you were a hungry greenhorn. Familiarity also breeds misfortune. I'm thankful that I can get away from that. None of it matters to me. I'm the guy who swings his leg over the arm of the chair.

The Real Me is born and reborn when I walk into the office, give instructions to the secretaries, and preside over the conference table around which my associates have been waiting.

I address them with the familiar *tú*.

They address me with formal *usted*.

(Authority accrues certain privileges.)

They stand at attention when I enter a room.

I remain seated until they've all left.

I never leave to go to the bathroom.

I urinate before a meeting.

I do not drink water during a meeting.

They do. They condemn themselves in my presence by acknowledging their *needs*. (Words, class indicators. They *need*. I *have*.)

And so, imagine my surprise (concealed as it was by my best poker face) on that January 6, when my colleagues welcomed me to the conference room wearing dark sunglasses.

I gave no signs of surprise beyond the aforementioned, failed joke.

I dealt with old business, asked for opinions, gave permission to go to the restroom, offered water, as if this were business as usual . . .

The meeting ended. That was Friday. I announced a meeting for Monday, wondering what would happen. Everyone stood but me.

On Monday my employees again showed off their dark sunglasses. And they showed something more troubling: an inquisitive audacity. Behind the dark lenses, I imagined their defiant stares masking fear. Their isolation from me was at once a barrier to overcome and an opportunity to seize. My antennae vibrated as I perceived a shift of power. The power of the weakness that I imposed on them. The weakness of the power that they returned to me. When one of them rose and left for the restroom, I noticed for the first time the creaking of floorboards. I pressed my legs together.

What was happening?

I wasn't about to let them explain the situation to me. I moved on with a vertiginous feeling, as though I was walking along the edge of an abyss. My associates' attitude, whether rebellious or disrespectful, was so unbearable that it forced my hand. Without considering the consequences, I gave an order.

"Take off your glasses, comets. The sun is out."

They all looked at me with astonishment.

I knew that I had won this game.

This office rebellion had shattered a piece of the security with which, until then, I had governed them and in governing them, I had governed myself.

The insubordinates kept their dark sunglasses on.

But that's another story.

7

Everybody needs comfort. The stray dog seeks a master to rescue him, bathe him, and take care of him: food and shelter, even more precious to those who depend on the kindness of others. The caged bird appreciates its birdseed but yearns for the freedom to fly; when it escapes and flies away, it yearns for the never-ending supply of birdseed. According to popular wisdom, teenagers rebel against their parents, go out into the world, and return, contrite, begging for shelter, food, comfort, and unconditional affection. This was the case of an old friend of mine, Abel Pagán, who rebelled, left home, and was forced by circumstance to return humbled. Nobody knows how things will turn out. I have everything I need right now. But how about Mexico? If the peso's devalued? If the drug traffickers take over? If the city floods once and for all, the shit rising to the Heights? If the highways become impassable and filled with bandits, the way they were in the nineteenth century? If Zapata rises from the dead? If the captured legendary soldier Valentín, as in the equally legendary *corrido*, refuses to talk? If the fat lady sings? If the next big earthquake leaves the country in ruins? . . .

Dog, bird, child, this evening I approach the house where L lives.

I have no desire to show my wounds. I relax and am, as always, whole, affectionate, personable, without visible scars, without unnecessary explanations, because I follow the saying so little appreciated by Latin American women who are cheated on and by the men who cheat on them: *Never complain. Never explain.*

L never asks for explanations and has never heard me complain. That's our arrangement. L is just a mix of lovely attributes, forgivable pettiness, and understandable vices, and gives me so much that I cannot credit a single defect. L is aware of them and flaunts them.

Does L wear those imperfections as so many badges of honor?

L bores easily, so needs entertainment and frequent surprises. In order to love another person, L says, you have to love yourself first. L loves L. L's not afraid to show weakness out of the belief that if our lovers know who we are, the possibility of astounding them increases because they are not expecting surprises. I have to let myself be deciphered, but not to tell all, so that I might not just be loved but also be loved for the things that I have not yet revealed.

L wants to be a mystery, and for me to be a mystery, too.

I know more or less zilch about L. We're like in the song: "*Don't talk to me anymore, let me imagine that the past doesn't exist and in the moment we met, we were born.*"

I know nothing about L except for what I know about our life ever since "*the moment we met,*" and L knows only the same about me, as well as the part of my life that's in the public domain. When I offer myself to L, there is an opaque curtain drawn over my life before my marriage to Priscila, when the baking family put me on the national stage. That's something L and I have in common. We love each other here and now, without any reference to our pasts. We don't discuss lovers, children, or ambitions, and we don't make promises. Our relationship exists in the here and now. While I sometimes give in to the temptation of memory, that only happens in my secret, unpublishable communication—*with you*, reader.

Unpublishable? What possessed me to say such a thing?

I allow myself to be surprised.

L must be aware of my public position but never mentions it, which makes me feel like a new man every time I come over, willing to renew myself on these nights of untold love with L, who does not know my family situation beyond what everybody knows (my marriage to the Queen of Spring in the house of the King of Bakery). The facts are irrelevant to a free spirit like L.

A free spirit? Can such a thing exist? Is there a single human being who is not tied, in some way, to his or her past and origin and family? Or to his or her profession, job, responsibility?

Yes, there is such a free spirit, a free spirit whose name is L. That's what I believe.

I do not know anything about L's past (*cue bolero*), nor do I want to know. Even if I did want to know, I couldn't find out, and not just because L knows how to keep a secret. L is a secret. Everything that L says and does is spontaneous, without precedent (or at least without any significant precedent). I've never come across anyone who lives so *completely* for the moment. And in spite of that, L has eyes full of wisdom, gestures connoting experience, and words that draw from a well of mystery. But none of these qualities can be attributed to a past that doesn't exist, because in each moment, L assumes that the past is present, and that the future is as well. I mean, when L remembers, what is important is not the memory, but the fact of remembering right now. And if L desires, this desire takes place in the here and now. L cancels out the past and the future, combining them into an eternal present: here and now, everything here and now, with an intensity that not only explains L, but that explains me, my passion for this unique being who takes me out of the ridiculous comedy of my household and the funereal solemnity of my office to place me in the radical moment—so beautiful, so rare, so everything!—in which I am with L, alive with L, in love with L.

Here and now all the problems, obligations, and ridiculousness of private life, and all the masquerades of public life, disappear. L redeems me, returns me to myself, to that part of my person that would otherwise remain hidden, latent, and perhaps lost forever.

I breathe into L's ear, while we hold each other close, and L breathes into my mouth. Life not only returns, it has been here all along, and I don't know what keeps me from abandoning everything to give myself unconditionally and without guilt to L's love.

8

Love interrupted. I chose L's apartment. Requirements: a place where I could come and go without being seen, centrally located, yet isolated. Result: a downtown building letting out onto a narrow alley on Oslo Street between Nice and Copenhagen.

Context: the Zona Rosa district, motley crowds day and night, distractions. Actions: leave the car on Hamburg Street. Walk a couple of blocks hidden among the crowds, knowing that the best disguise is oneself. I appear so often on TV, in the newspapers, and at public events, that nobody would suspect that the ordinary guy walking alone between Genoa and Antwerp streets is me.

It's a gamble.

And it's paid off. Until this night I had excitedly planned to enjoy with L.

Somebody recognizes me, says hello, stops me.

"Sir! It's you!"

Then everybody else recognizes me.

"What an honor!"

"What a thrill!"

"Can I have your autograph?"

"A man of the people!"

"A regular guy!"

"Not at all, not at all," I say, moving my hands to indicate a total lack of pretension, an impervious will, a normality, "not at all, not at all, like any other citizen, walking around, watching the world, you know. Living locked up in an office surrounded by bodyguards makes you lose touch, get self-important. I have to step out a little, anonymously, with other people, like you. Thank you, great to meet you, now I have to run, they're waiting for me, see you later, see you soon!"

"What a modest guy!"

"What a democrat!"

I knew I would eventually be recognized in the Zona Rosa. I have to skip going to L's alley on Oslo and instead return to the parking lot in front of the Bellinghausen restaurant and from there head back home.

What awaits me there?

On this night that I had set aside to be with L, returning instead to Lomas Virreyes, I happen onto a huge family fight. Don Celestino, flying into a rage (or a rage flying into him, because our vices and virtues precede and survive us), rebukes his son Abelardo in the middle of the living room. Poor Priscila whimpers halfway up the staircase, and stoic but disappointed (or the other way around), I enter the house at the worst possible moment.

"You're a drone!" shouts Don Celes. "You just want to bum around at my expense."

"No, that's not what I'm saying," says Abelardo calmly. "I want to pursue my vocation."

"Vocation, vocation! There is no vocation here. Vocation is a vacation," exclaims Don Celes with a literary turn of phrase that I didn't think he had in him. "Here we do our jobs. Here we work hard. Here there's a fortune that has to be managed."

"But father, that's not my vocation."

"Of course it isn't your vocation, you little bum, it's your *obligation*. Do you understand? We all have ob-li-ga-tions. We don't screw around here! This is no joke! So just stop this talking this nonsense!"

Don Celes mocks the young man by affecting the manner of a dandy or a fop, though he mostly succeeds in making himself seem a cretin . . .

"But of course!" he clucks, sprinkling an imaginary handkerchief. "The young gentleman excuses himself from labor. The *señorito* has, listen to this, a *vo-ca-tion*. The little lord of the manor refuses to work—"

"No father, I am not refusing to—"

"Hush, you insolent brat! I am speaking!"

"And I am right."

"What did you say? You're what? What . . . ? Do my ears deceive me?"

"I don't want to run a business. I want to be a writer."

"You what? You want to what? And what will you be able to afford to eat, scoundrel? Alphabet soup? Paper enchiladas? A *mole* sauce made of ink? Who are you making fun of, Don Shakespearito? Show a little more respect to your lord father, the man who raised you, yes sir, who gave you everything, an education, a roof over your head, and clothing, to whom you come now with this nonsense about wanting to be a wrrrri-ter! Little Don Fauntleroy, tell me, do I have the word *idiot* written across my forehead?"

"I'm not asking you for anything."

"You don't need to. I already gave you everything. And this is how you pay me back, you miserable parasite!"

"Verbena!" Priscila says timidly from the fourth step of the staircase. "Doves!"

Nobody pays her any mind. "You ought to learn from your brother-in-law Adam" (That's me and now I am a weapon).

"I admire Adam," Abelardo dares to comment.

"Good! Because Adam married your sister so he could move up in the world; he hit the jackpot; he was Mr. Nobody, a beggar, not a pot to piss in, and you see, he knew how to take advantage of my position and my fortune, the rascal! He knew how to move up, and he got to where he is because he married your sister . . ."

"Hymen," Priscila moans skillfully, but nobody pays her any mind.

"And look at him now: he's a big shot, he's the cream of the crop. Aren't you ashamed of yourself? Aren't you embarrassed?"

"I am not—" Abelardo mutters.

"You're not anything, you're nothing," Don Celes says raising his hand in a threatening manner. "You're not what?" he asks without making any sense. "You—?" he interrupts himself when he turns to see me looking at him sternly, unapologetically. I walk over to Abelardo and offer him my hand.

"Don't let yourself be humiliated, my brother-in-law."

"I'm not . . ." he stammers.

"Hold onto your self-respect."

"I . . ."

"Move on from this house. Make your own way."

"You . . ."

"Nothing. Expect nothing from me. You'll make your own way in the world."

My words silence the family.

With my usual self-restraint, I avoid all stares. I am my own boss. No quarreling. No mocking. No patronizing airs. No triumphalism. Don Celes is frozen into a statue. Priscila is cold and motionless. Abelardo is struggling between a kind smile and a grateful embrace.

I'd only intervened in the first place because I was recognized in the street and couldn't go where I wanted to be, in L's arms.

Priscila slaps the maid across the face as she carries a tray upstairs, announcing the resumption of normal life.

9

"Adam, did you see?"

"What?"

"That boy."

"What boy?"

"The Boy-God."

"The boy *what*?"

He appeared where he was least expected, I am told by L, who along with my secretaries, keeps me apprised of the human-interest news that isn't reported on in the briefings I receive.

At the intersection of Quintana Roo and Insurgentes Avenue. He stands on a little platform, dominating the traffic on the avenue. And it's not some open space, but full of fast-moving cars except when there're those horrible traffic jams, and it's all impatient honks and insults. It's a place where arteries converge, and where impatient speed alternates with even more impatient gridlock.

"You've got to see him—I went to see him," L said. "Stopping traffic, wearing a white tunic, standing on his box like that desert hermit on his pillar, remember that Buñuel film? No? Well, it was Saint Simeon preaching in the desert: his congregation was dwarves, his mother, and the Devil. But this child addresses the traffic of Insurgentes and Quintana Roo, and what's remarkable, Adam, is that first people honk their horns at him, but then they stop, get out of their cars, make fun of him, tell him to burn in hell for causing a traffic jam, I'm running late, get out of the way you little pipsqueak . . ."

"Pipsqueak?"

"He can't be older than eleven, Adam. You've got to see him . . ."

"I see him in your eyes. What'd he give you, a little loco weed?"

"Come on Adam, I'm being serious. First the drivers were all pissed off. Then some of them start paying attention to him. It's like he mesmerizes them, you know what I mean?"

I gestured that I didn't, but listened attentively to that story . . .

"Attention," L repeated. "You know? I just realized that our great defect is that we don't pay attention."

"L, don't lose your thread. Get on with your story."

"It's my story, okay. We don't pay attention to others. We don't pay attention to *ourselves*. We let things happen like the wind blowing—am I right?—and other people happen by."

I asked if that entire speech was a way of reproaching me for not knowing that there was a preacher on the corner of Insurgentes and . . .

"An eleven-year-old preacher."

"Right."

"A Boy-God."

"You're talking nuts."

"But I'm not nuts. You have to listen to me, because you can't go there to see what's happening. I can. Nobody knows me from . . . nobody recognizes me."

If this was a reproach about having to be a secret lover, the reproach did not register with me at the time.

"What does he say?"

"Stop running around, that's mainly what he says. Don't rush. Where are you going in such a hurry? Where's the fire? Can't you just wait one single minute? Don't you want to hear the voice of God?

"At first they heckled the Boy. Until that child's gaze silenced the crowd.

"If only you could have seen him, Adam. His very gaze conferred authority. It was a gaze full of veiled threats. A loving gaze, too. A powerful love mixed with a great authority and a trace of menace. All this in a ten- or eleven-year-old boy."

"Is he blond? Ugly?" I said, wanting to lower L's admiring tone, which was getting on my nerves.

"He's, I don't know, luminous. Yes. He shines, but it's like he really sees us."

"Rhymes with *Jesus*," I tried to joke.

"No, no, no, no," L said, "not that, that would be like a parody, wouldn't it? No, this child isn't God, he's not Jesus, he is, I don't know, Adam. What's the word? He's a *messenger . . .*"

"How do you know?"

"Adam. He had *wings* on his ankles. Wings on his ankles. You see where I'm going with this?"

"Yes, not very far. Anybody can glue a pair of little wings to their ankles, to their back, to their . . ."

"But nobody admits it . . ."

I gave her a questioning look.

"He took off the wings from his feet, do you hear me?"

"So even he admits he's a fraud."

"Just the opposite! He said that he was a schoolboy. He would go to school every morning, where he learned to read, to write, to sing, to do math, and to draw. But after school, he would transform. He followed his heart, he said, and he'd put on the white gown, and stick the little wings to his ankles, and put on the wig of golden curls, and he'd go preach at this intersection of busy avenues, nobody told him to do it, just his heart, the need of his soul, he said, he was a schoolboy, nothing more, he was not deceiving anybody, he would rather go play marbles, but he did what he had to do, not because he had to obey an order, but because *he could follow no other path*, that's what he told us."

"Us? Are we many?"

"The crowd is bigger every afternoon, Adam. Haven't you heard?"

"You know very well that I don't communicate well with the city authorities."

"Well, you should hear about it. You don't trust the city? Then believe me, baby. I'm telling you what I saw."

10

Abelardo moved out of his father's house, and when I saw him, he told me the following:

My cousin Sonsoles, sucking on her Mimi lollipop and prancing around, told me that someone had telephoned on behalf of the poet Maximino Sol. He wanted to meet me and would be expecting me at his house in the Condesa neighborhood at five. I went to the audience feeling ill at ease: Maximino Sol was a great writer; he also exerted a fascinating sort of tyranny over Mexican literature, monopolizing the publication of magazines and, through his disciples and close friends, the book reviews in newspapers. I went there, I admit, fascinated, resisting an impulse to rebel by admitting that pride, while a virtue, was also an extravagance for an unknown poet. Maximino Sol received me in his wood-paneled office, where he introduced me to a thirty-year-old man with blood-shot eyes and a mustache in the style of the writer Valle Arizpe or some colonial Kaiser. I identified him as the poet's notorious enforcer, who in proud cynicism, signed his attacks against Sol's enemies as "Luna," the moon, while Sol, the sun, atop the lyrical Olympus, beatifically feigned ignorance of his satellites tumbling around madly in the lower depths. A sidekick to his boss, a parasite on others, he would forever be someone's servant; as a servant to money and power, he would never exist on his own account. I pictured this assistant, slightly overweight at the hips, sporting a ruff and holding a quill pen at the ready, waiting to take dictation of every word pronounced by the poet who, with old-fashioned Mexican courtesy, received me in a three-piece suit, a white shirt, and a thick silk necktie fastened with a tiepin. The poet's body, tiny and chubby, looked constrained in the gray pinstriped vest, and his double chin hung a bit over the knot of his tie. The vest, instead of tightening the body, was tightened by the body, so that Maximino Sol seemed put together from two perfect circles, the double-chin giving rise to the belly that seemed to emerge from the neck, and vice versa. But the leonine head concentrated all the energy that was absent in the flabby body, and his carefully ruffled mane gave him a fierce air, emphasized by the mixture of impatience and disdain in his gaze. Nevertheless, an angelic veil magically covered all of Maximino Sol's manners and movements.

He sat down and told me that my little poem published in *K*____ magazine had come to his attention. There was perhaps too much influence from Neruda and Lorca—he said while smiling cherubically—and he suggested, in any case, that I choose instead models like Jorge Guillén and Emilio Prados, whom one could paraphrase without being too obvious. In any case, he went on, mimicry is inevitable in literature and, after all, to choose one's mentors well is a sign of talent.

The amanuensis passed an open copy of the magazine to the poet.

"You have talent," the poet said, leafing kindly through the pages where I had imprinted my literary baby steps. "And besides, you are young . . ."

Sitting uncomfortably before the great man, I felt even less comfortable in my soul than in my body. Before acknowledging the compliment, I examined the rich mahogany of the office, I admired the perfect order of the bookshelves, and I tried to amuse myself by speculating about the way the poet organized his books: by genre, alphabetical or chronological order, or a combination of all these? I let my mind wander to distract myself from the obvious: I was being recruited so that my youth and talent would join, as he would soon inform me, the writers of *K____* magazine, directed by Maximino Sol. The poet's discourse had been directed to a conscript. His affable smile and his alert eyes told me, without words, that a great honor was being done to me, and that is how I understood it.

"Thank you," I said.

But the association of my youth (verifiable) and my talent (still questionable) in one equation, made me uncomfortable, especially when Sol went off on a long disquisition about the lack of real minds in our literature.

He recalled everybody: the poets—Alfonso Reyes, Salvador Novo, Xavier Villaurrutia, Jaime Torres Bodet, Jorge Cuesta, Gilberto Owen, José Gorostiza, Carlos Pellicer, and even Tablada, Urbina, González Martínez—and a few novelists—Azuela, Guzmán, Muñoz, Ferretis, Magdaleno. Sol began by dispatching, one by one, the writers of his generation, of previous generations, and then of generations younger than his own. In Olympian style he conferred prizes and punishments, granting this poet a second place, those two a third, the one over there an honorable mention, the vast majority a failing grade, and one, his mortal enemy, was flat-out sent to stand in the corner with donkey ears and the impenitent heretic's dunce cap. In any case the mediocre or bad poets sat in the front rows and the novelists, considered more or less the mentally disabled of literature, in the last.

I wondered, as I listened to Sol talk, what place he would grant me, especially when I ceased to be young and had my own body of work. I understood as well what place Maximino Sol awarded himself in this perpetual classroom without recess or vacation, in which, or so it seemed, the teacher was also the prized student.

"What is being written today is not especially interesting. But we must have confidence in the young. In reality, the places are vacant: the first rows, unoccupied. Only the young, in time, can fill them."

He paused magisterially and cordially invited me to join his magazine. He did not have to say what we both knew: this was the only path by which I could become a recognized poet.

I pictured myself back in school with the teacher. Since my schooldays were not far behind, I was able to ask myself with enough spontaneity: was I going to spend my life waiting for Maximino Sol to pass or fail me, waiting for an A, a C, an F, or an exemplary punishment after class; write on the blackboard a hundred times, *There is nothing in Mexican literature except the work of Maximino Sol?*

I told him that perhaps he was right, I was too young, and at my age I could do without any kind of mentorship until . . .

He brusquely interrupted me. He said that youth was not eternal and that lyrical energy was lost if it was not channeled.

"I am disciplined, maestro," I said, without gauging the ambiguity of the appeal.

Halfway between flattered and annoyed, he added that Mexico was a country of sacrifices, and that those who showed talent were quickly attacked until they were dead.

"If you stick your head out, they will cut it off."

Talent—no matter how much you have—is not enough, he went on, without a shield to protect it. That is what a magazine is, and that is what a group and a teacher are: the protection of the seed constantly threatened by envy and overwhelming controversies; threatened by chauvinists if the young poet demonstrates his inevitable universal learning; threatened by cosmopolitans if, on the contrary, he shows, as it were, his folkloric garments; threatened by the political commitment demanded by the left and by the artistic purity demanded by the right . . . How was I going to survive alone, so young, so talented, so . . . ?

I feared, listening to him, watching him say all of this with an almost evangelical concern for my poor person, that he would see in me and in my probable work only a youthful poetry that, extolling early experience and vitality, would serve the old man of letters to moralize before his contemporaries, making them feel guilty that they had lost what Maximino Sol, vicariously protecting a young author, still had: precisely this initial vitality, the experience of wonder. I felt exposed by a manipulation that offered me immediate protection and eventual glory in exchange for my adherence to a hierarchy presided over by the Sol; a hierarchy of values, texts, interests . . . I felt chosen to justify the demands of the pope of a literary chapel before his rival pontiffs. I pictured a court in which our youth was the indispensable support for the continued demands of an old writer before the adult world: "Look,

I have more young writers around me than anybody else, and these young poets exalt me and denigrate you, my rivals . . ."

"I would like to hear my own voice," I said naïvely.

Maximino Sol abstained from laughing. He said seriously:

"The 'I' is an 'us' or it is not."

In my turn, I abstained from laughing at the sophism, but the poet continued: "Our group, our magazine, we constitute a chorus. Outside of it, Abelardo, all is cacophony."

"Abelardo," he repeated, tilting his head as though to excuse himself, "may I call you that?" There was only one step left: he would address me in the familiar *tú*. For some reason, I felt repugnance toward any familiarity with him, and especially toward the assistant who, standing, exchanged glances of infinite patience with his boss. I never saw a less desperate person than that man. In him, waiting was everything, but what was he waiting for? I thought of him, in spite of his appearance, as The Desperate One. But even that—desperation—was taken away from him, with the quick and fractured imagination that accompanied this interview, by the literary pope who was taking shape, this time slowly and seamlessly, before my very eyes. However, the relationship between the two— Maximino Sol and his secretary—seemed perfectly normal to me in the hierarchy of subordination, until the man slightly wider at the waist dared to say to me:

"Don't be a total idiot, *tú*. Maximino Sol, no less, offers you glory, and you reject it. Do you imagine that you'll get anywhere in Mexico without him?"

"Are you saying that you depend on him completely?" I answered. "Well, I don't."

"Shut up," Sol said to him as a prelude to a tantrum and a symphony of facial tics that momentarily paralyzed the secretary.

"No, maestro, it's just that this guy in no way deserves to be here, nor is he worthy of your even looking at him. I don't know why you insist on casting pearls before—"

"I said shut up!" repeated the poet, this time with a full show of furious authority.

"Okay, maestro, just don't yell at me."

"I will yell at you as much as I wish," said the poet, now very cool and calm with his angelic smile, this time directed at me.

I understood that this charade consisted in showing me what my future would be if I did not accept the offer of protection in exchange for submission that I was being offered.

I stood up and was about to turn my back on them and walk out, but in Maximino Sol's light-colored eyes, aged rivals of my own, I read such hatred and confusion that I knew, as Sol spoke to me, I would need to speak up for myself.

"Young man, I have a voice. You are right, at least about that. I will survive those whom you consider my flatterers. I have a voice," he repeated, whether to convince me or to convince himself, I don't know.

I was able to say what I wanted to say: "Because you hear other voices."

"Well, you know, there are a lot of deaf people in this world."

"Maybe you're one of them, if you're unaware that the voice you hear is also heard by, I don't know, a driver, a baker, a housewife."

"Your populism moves me. Offer it to the late Mr. Neruda. A baker or a driver doesn't create poetry."

"But at least they create something."

I was going to say, they lulled a child to sleep, they insulted an arrogant person, they loved a woman, but I recalled the more intimate, and therefore more public tones, of Maximino Sol's poetry, the tenderness of his violence, the strangeness of the unfinished symbols that he pitted against all the finished religious, political, and economic signs in the world, and I pleaded, dear God, let me be like that man's poetry, but not like the man himself; dear father, don't let me sacrifice everything to literary opportunism and glory; give me a corner, dear mother, where I can value a son, a wife, and a friend more than all the laurels of the earth; save me from the bootlickers, Lord, and help me acquire my youth with age, instead of losing it with time.

When I left the office, closing the door and entering a vestibule with purplish leaded windows, I heard Maximino Sol's prickly, temperamental, exalted voice, without low tones, scolding his secretary. I couldn't make out the words, but I thought it would be funny to come back with a blank book and offer it to the shrewdness of this man condemned to the treachery of his flatterers and blind to the independence of his friends. Please, I prayed again, don't let me grow old like that. Let me depend on a woman, a son, and a friend, not on literary ties and vanity. Glory is the mask of death. It has no progeny.

Abelardo fell silent.

I only remarked: "Read the writers, but don't get to know them in person."

11

You know that strip of land underneath the bridge, Mr. Gorozpe? You ought to pay a visit. I bet you'd recognize some of the people camping there. Some of them, they used to go to parties or even get their picture in the newspapers, you know, the style pages. Graduations. Saint Days. Sporting events. Vacations in Acapulco, Tequesquitengo, or at the very least, in Nautla. Now look at them in their tents. See how the wind lashes the canvas. See how the rain leaks through. Just look at them now. Thank goodness they brought portable toilets. Just look. Chamber pots, they've always been around. Before, only people on their last legs wound up out here. Now people live here who used to vacation in Acapulco, or at the very least Nautla. They all used to be in the newspapers; now they lie down on gutted sofas. They used to chill cans in their fridges. Now they collect cans, supposedly for recycling, but they sell bags full of cans for scrap. Same difference. You ought to see for yourself. Gutted sofas. Remember that family? Now they're all alcoholics. Out of total desperation. To numb themselves. To forget. To . . . But not everybody lets themselves go to seed, you know? Even down there, some of them show a little initiative. They defend themselves with kidnapped dogs, pit bulls mostly. Spiked collars. Chained beasts. Set free only to defend them. The more enterprising ones built a fence out of chains. They try to defend themselves and all those who have also fallen. Old colleagues. Family. Friends. Then one day: poor. Camped out here, you know, in Taco Flats? That's what they named the place: Taco Flats! They put up the chain barrier to defend themselves, to maintain the illusion that, although they're down, they are defending themselves behind a *chain* barrier, just like the old days when they built walls around their houses. They couldn't, Mr. Gorozpe, they just couldn't put up any resistance. They thought they could keep out others who were even more downtrodden than they were, mark the boundaries of their own exclusive community of misery, misery reserved for them alone. But Mr. Gorozpe, they couldn't, they just couldn't pull it off. Yesterday's poor were already there. Only today's poor didn't notice them. They just arrived. They drew a line around a zone of misfortune. They set up tents, toilets, dogs, gutted sofas. But they didn't look carefully. The people who were already down and out were already there. But the new poor, the new down-and-out, didn't even look at them, and only after they locked themselves in behind their chain barrier with their dogs did they realize that none of their initiative would do them any good. Because the old poor were already there. Only the new poor hadn't seen them. They were already *inside*, do you follow me?"

"Why are you talking in the plural?"

"Why am I what, sir?"

"Yes, of course, you are. You sound like you're talking about a lot of people."

"It's just that—"

"It's just that nothing. I only gave you orders to ruin the family of—"

47

"Of course, I'm talking about them."

"Don't tell me that you broke more than one family?"

"It's just that—"

"What?"

"It's just that one can't be too discriminating in that—"

"So you threw out the baby with the bathwater?"

"Mr. Adam Góngora doesn't discriminate. So what happened is that the entire block ended up in Taco Flats, the entire block of rich folks . . . Mr. Góngora says that ought to teach them a lesson."

"Oh."

"And I said that Taco Flats was gringo-lingo. Better they should call them *Gorozpevilles*."

"How's that?"

"Like in honor of you."

12

Sometimes I have no choice but to steel myself and take part in the life of high society. What else can I do? And what a drag. But if I never show myself, people will think that I don't exist anymore. I mean, if I don't show my face in society. Because to let myself be seen at dinners, parties, weddings, and baptisms is the best— sometimes the only—way to prove my own existence. On these occasions, I run into ex-presidents everybody thought were dead; millionaires of yesteryear who made their fortunes when Mexican capitalism was young; secretaries of state of dubious reputation; debutantes who became society ladies, matrons of a certain age, or as the men call them, croissants.

I have an advantage: I don't see anybody. I am known by hearsay. Although I appear in the newspaper and on TV, I'm all but a state secret. I rarely go to private events, but each time I do, I make sure that my wife accompanies me to reinforce the notion of my character: Gorozpe is rarely seen because he works so much, but he's just a person like all of us. Just look at his wife. When she was young she was very famous for being—

"Queen of Spring . . ."

"The Princess of the Carnival of Veracruz . . ."

"And of Mazatlán . . ."

"Pretty . . ."

"Cute . . ."

"Pleasant looking."

"No offense intended, but she really let herself go."

"No, she's still a fox."

"Oh my, Marylou, did you call her an ox?"

"Well, she is a little chubby . . . pleasantly plump, that is."

"Not so much in her body—"

"In her face. She looks like cherry pie."

"You mean like the dough for the pie before it goes in the oven."

"Did you see her little eyes? Her—"

"See? I don't think she can see anything. Look at those tiny little eyes, so close together, lost in the flour dough of that huge face—"

"Put your shears away, Sofonisba, here comes the couple . . ."

"How lovely!"

"How delightful!"

I can read lips. I warn you. From far away. From the moment I walk into a living room, I read what the tongues are wagging. It's not hard. They always say the same things. I only put the words in their mouths that are always there. Funny, what I imagine them saying corresponds to the movements of their lips. They don't say anything about me. Men are immune, rock to shears. More likely my presence puts them in a position in which they must not show surprise at my being there, as rare as my presence is, sometimes with many months between appearances . . . I can count my annual outings in high society on one hand. I realize that they all have an *idea* about who I am based on my *public* persona. In other words, they have an *idea* about me prior to my arrival, prior to being in my physical *presence*. I'm already a *figure* of newspapers, television, magazines, so I do not cause surprise. I'm a familiar *effigy* that everyone is used to, and my physical *presence* doesn't alter their prior *perception* of *me*.

For this reason, all stares directed at us as a couple home in on Priscila alone. She often attends these sorts of parties without me. The memory of her youthful fame (the Queen of And So On) has faded, and instead her social presence only recalls how much life has changed her, the loss of her princessly freshness (Carnival, Spring) and her current plumpness. I have changed very little since I became famous. White hairs on my temples, but natural ones, not whitewashed like those of Mexican cinema's mature heartthrobs. I still have my hair and my features are regular: wide forehead, scant eyebrows (I only dye them a little), an inquisitive and therefore interesting nose, lips that neither show smiles nor betray anger or any feeling whatsoever. And a cleft chin that gives me the natural look of gallantry that I neither seek nor impose.

I exercise my gaze. I veil it. I concentrate it. I never soften it. With it I threaten, warn, disdain, attract if necessary, and reject if I can do so without being feckless. Adam Gorozpe's gaze, the male gaze on steroids. No wonder nobody speaks when I arrive at a dinner at the house of the old minister Don Salvador Ascencio, to whom I owe a favor or two (and I don't like to appear ungrateful). Nobody speaks. They all look at me. They all make way for me even if they've already given a wide berth to the ocean liner christened the Queen Priscila. It is not the same thing. They *let her pass*. For me, *they gangway*.

But as they gangway for me, none of the people gathered here—

forgotten politicians, the young ladies of yesteryear who are the old ladies of today, anonymous individuals whose names and positions I couldn't care less about—step aside, that is they can't get away from me. This is part of my strategy, I confess to you, my faithful listeners, to let myself be seen often on the news but very seldom at parties. They simply can't get away from me. They move around me. They return to me until the moment I leave.

You figure that these interactions are a huge pain? You figure right. That's why I arrange my life around bureaucratic, corporate, and political work, where my word is law (though, why did they greet me on Three Kings Day with dark sunglasses?), and around my domestic relations with my father-in-law, the King of Bakery, and his tantrums and with my wife Priscila and her verbal inconsequentialities. And what about my brother-in-law Abelardo? What happened to him? When he left the house, I confess, I lost the only useful handle by which I could take hold of the mansion of Lomas Virreyes, even the rooms of the late Mamacita And-So-On's all-pink-except-for-the-iron-bidet décor, rest her soul, the house in which I had chosen to live because there I could comfortably live a life of habit and repetition without being disturbed, a life I could take or leave, and a life which, as a bonus, would advertise my devotion to family.

"Adam Gorozpe lives with his father-in-law."

"He has from the beginning."

"When he was a nobody."

"Shut up!"

"He lives with his wife."

"The sweetheart of his youth."

"'Youth, divine treasure—'"

"'Already gone, never to return.' Ha!"

"And a very strange brother-in-law."

"Sort of a boho, no?"

"Not what you'd call a serious young man—"

"One who knows his own mind."

Living in my father-in-law's house helps to conceal my identity, making me seem a frugal man, concentrated on his work, faithful to his family . . .

They're not aware of my other life.

They don't know that there is L.

13

Here are assorted recent events my secretaries have conveyed to me from the *Mexicomedy*:

An old lady was traveling peacefully on the bus that runs from Salto del Agua to Ciudadela to Rayón. A young man boarded the bus, and, with gun in hand, ordered the passengers to hand over their wallets, rings, and sunglasses. He extended a garishly colored baseball cap to collect the items. When he approached the old lady, she grabbed the cap from him, emptied the contents, and then beat the young robber with that same cap, addressing him as a beggar, a petty thief, a scoundrel, and an insolent brat, as well as a naughty little rascal and other old fashioned expressions that betrayed the lady's age. The surprised young man first covered his head against the old lady's onslaught. Then she let go of the cap and beat him with an umbrella until the little thief jumped from the vehicle, stumbled, and fell headfirst. Everyone laughed in relief. Who was the brave little old lady? She said her name was Sara García.

An obscure artist created an inflatable sculpture of Dumbo the elephant on the roof of his Yucatan Avenue house. The statue broke free from its ties and flew over nearby San Martín Park, where it killed an unsuspecting couple. "Elephants are contagious," the artist said, by way of excusing himself.

Luxury items are being sold at lowered prices: sunglasses, Audis, Porsches, Rolex, Cartier rings, Mont Blanc pens, Prada bags, Zegna shirts, Gucci shoes, Cavalli dresses, and so on. The ad reads: "Better prices for a better image."

Exports of *chilaquiles* have risen ninety-two percent. Nobody can explain who, or why anyone, abroad is buying pieces of hard tortilla, but nowadays they come with recipes to make sauces and instructions to season them according to the consumer's taste. The ad says: "Be patriotic. Export a *chilaquil*."

As North American tourism diminishes, Chinese tourism increases. When questioned, the visitors speak about the similarities between Chinese and Mexican cuisine—spicy, small, varied dishes, ideal for each to create a menu to his or her own taste. The surprising truth is that, regardless of what they say, these tourists only eat what they export to us. We asked the minister in charge: Is this good for foreign commerce? We are still waiting for his answer.

Candelaria the Gondolier gives an interview in which she confesses that she was the mistress of some dozen drug traffickers. She was passed from hand to hand. They killed one another. She survived and waited for her next lover. She says that she lived on an islet of Xochimilco, surrounded by flowers and piglets and passing tourist gondolas in the canals. "I guess I'm just bucolic," she explains.

Yasmine Sulimán, a political refugee who fled from a murderous regime in the Middle East, found work in the José Vasconcelos Library of Mexico City, and moved into a nearby apartment on Mystery Lane (continuation of Reforma). She was murdered yesterday by a crazy library patron who asked her for the complete works of Augusto Monterroso. When he received the book it was so slim that he became enraged and strangled Yasmine.

Sixth grader Jenaro González has admitted to being the Boy-God who preaches on Sundays at the intersection of Insurgentes and Quintana Roo. Our reporters followed him home from the evening assembly then lost him. The next morning they picked up his trail and confronted him at his school on Chapultepec Avenue. The young boy confessed to being the child preacher. All he does is put on a wig of golden curls and a little white robe, and he walks barefoot. In fact, he has porcupine hair and swears that he does what he does following a divine mandate, even if later he can't remember what he preached. Our clever reporter interviewed him again on Chapultepec this week. The boy with spiky hair repeated this story. But at that precise moment, the Boy-God was preaching to a crowd at the intersection of Insurgentes and Quintana Roo, thus exposing Jenato González as an impostor. Unsolvable mystery?

Our lost cities—of the type called *callampas* in Chile, *villas miseria* in Argentina, *favelas* in Brazil, *ranchitos* in Caracas, *Hoovervilles* in the Great Depression—have been baptized *Gorozpevilles*, (according to the secretaries) an insolent reference to me, Adam Gorozpe, to whom the surrounding poverty of Mexico City is groundlessly attributed, with the obvious aim of slandering and maligning me. There are now similarly lost cities on the outskirts of Guadalajara, Monterrey, Morelia, and Torreón. It is worth noting that centers of organized criminality as notorious as Juárez, Tijuana, and Tampico do not have these shanty towns and tent cities because the drug traffickers in those cities enforce a high degree of discipline that consists in making any non-regulated urban manifestation disappear from one day to the next. "*Gorozpevilles* damage our image," said Don Hipólito el de Santa, a blind old pianist and head of the Desert Cartel. Should one assume that the drug traffickers show respect toward a man of such honest reputation as me? It's an innocent question.

14

When we move from our bed to the world at large (from the bedroom to the boardroom in my case), we become aware of the price we must always pay for any joy we've experienced in our love life. Nobody willingly deprives himself of love (except, to an extent, masochists, who, after all, love their proud singularity; and sadists, who take their pleasure to extremes that might be harmful to others). Sometimes, love happens naturally without abuse or hardship. *We have been together since forever. Both our families predetermined our love. Who else would I marry but the saint of a girlfriend I've gone out with forever?* Through my Holguín connections, I know of marriages reminiscent of traditional Hindu practice, arranged when the bride and groom were still children. There are ugly young women who supposedly arrive at the wedding altar as virgins. There are others—I've surprised them behind curtains, in the backseats of cars, camouflaged by trees—usually with their official boyfriends, sometimes with men I don't know, who introduce themselves, sometimes proud, sometimes embarrassed, all of whom rush into nuptials and marry with their fictitious virginity intact.

Because a woman is supposed to be a virgin, whereas a man is not. The stud who shows up at his wedding as a virgin is more of a dud. We suspect him of being impotent, or of being gay and passing, or of convincing himself that he's straight; he could be latent, he could be a mama's boy. He could simply be chaste, shy, or unaware of a priestly vocation. On the other side of the aisle, the young woman who does not arrive a virgin is a shameless hussy. There are no excuses. The double standard is *the* standard. In any case, there are arranged marriages and love-matches that are paid for with undesirable consequences in social life. The horny teenager sleeps with the maid, but it never occurs to him—nor would he be allowed—to marry her. Besides, she would not be comfortable around people she was accustomed to serving, although there are cases, oh yes, there are cases . . . There are "distinguished" men married to women who are un-. When asked, they give *carnal* excuses—she satisfies him like no other woman can—but rarely *social* ones—she grew up poor, but thanks to me she has been elevated to a higher class.

In a conventional marriage like mine, there are no surprises. As I've already pointed out, Priscila is clueless; she says things she shouldn't say when she should say something else, or to play it safe, remain silent. I have already given enough examples to establish her lack of a compass. And whoever is listening to me already knows that my life with Priscila is a masquerade that I put on in order to become, in my public life, what I am not—nor do I care to be—in my private life. In a moment though, you'll learn how such a reliable situation can lead to unreliable situations.

Then, to repeat what you already know, there is my life with L, an extended pleasure that can be interrupted by spontaneous speeches that return me to non-erotic reality.

For example, L returns stoked from a Luismi concert at the National Auditorium. L's admiration for the singer is at once singular and plural. What L tells me about Luismi—he's so handsome, he sings so well, he sure can move—is all the more significant because ten thousand spectators felt the same way. I understand these collective frames of mind, they are also part of politics, and if in a Luismi concert they are harmless, they become dangerous when instead of a singer, there is a politician holding forth from a balcony and offering a crowd hopes as illusory as those Luismi whispers:

Lie to me

Lie to me some more

Because your wicked ways make me so happy . . .

I listen to L and congratulate myself on my own political discretion. Start adding up what you already know: I live in my father-in-law the King of Bakery's house; I have a long marriage with Priscila, the deposed Queen of Spring; I go from the house to the office and from the office to the house; I rarely attend social events . . .

I extend this discretion to my love life with L—private, satisfying, unmentionable—despite the occasional oddities that threaten to affect it but turn out to be no more than passing swallows.

"Why don't you shave under your arms?" L asked.

"What?"

"You could shave your armpits."

"What for, L?"

"To be just like me."

"But I want to be different."

"You mean you don't want to be like me?"

"I like you, understand? That's enough for me."

"But you don't want to be like me."

"No, I totally prefer the difference."

"It's a whim of mine. A tiny whim. This small."

"I can just picture myself with shaved armpits and then shaving my hairy chest, arms, legs . . ."

"And your back, bear cub, don't forget your back."

And then we kiss, and the argument is done.

Other times the fault is mine, usually a result of my legal training, which seems to confuse as much as to clarify. A surgeon cannot make a mistake: if he operates for appendicitis on a man with a toothache, his license is revoked. A lawyer, on the other hand, can lie in the sense that he knows his arguments are based on a fallacy that is useful to win a case, to deceive a fool, or to confuse an enemy.

"Where were you on Friday the ninth at six o'clock?"

"Friday the sixth at nine o'clock?"

"You're lying . . ."

"I mean, Friday the ninth at six?"

"You're contradicting yourself."

"You're confusing me, counselor."

"Why are you confused all of a sudden? What are you trying to hide?"

"Nothing, I swear."

"Keep your story straight. Why are you trying to deceive me?"

"I . . . ?"

That is why I can say to L, when I stand up for my right to ejaculate, that semen retention is toxic. I don't even abstain from saying it in Latin:

Semen retentus venenum est.

L doesn't care about my Latin expressions. L believes that the retention of semen causes an intense internal orgasm that is far more satisfying than my external spurt.

"Besides," L ventures, "to retain semen is a mark of sanctity."

I make a face of feigned surprise: "How would you know that?"

"Saints have semen, but they restrain themselves."

"You and I are no saintly couple, L. And about saints one can—"

"We can aspire to—"

"You're so boring."

"Humor me."

"Okay. Although I assure you that . . ."

I mention these little spats so that you'll understand what a good relationship I have with L and how we overcome all our differences without ever fighting. Have we done something wrong? Are arguments between couples the spice of love, the prelude to making up? Sex can either free or imprison the eternal savage that we all carry within.

I sometimes think that we are born savages who, if left to our own devices, would act like animals who want nothing more than to survive and to satisfy our instinctive, immediate desires. The philosopher of nature tells us there is no such creature, because natural man lived a life of kindness, whereas every step forward in society is a step toward crime, sin, and the need for prohibitive rules of conduct designed to tame the natural savages that we have been since our beginning.

It seems to me that as soon as he leaves behind the sylvan life to enter society, the savage murders his father and fornicates with his mother. Oedipus usually symbolizes this passage, which, regardless of what happens, imposes on us rules of conduct that we accept with heads hung in shame, because to break those rules would lead us to jail, the gallows, or at least social ostracism.

This myth, though, does little to explain the vicissitudes of love in society and its relationship to such dissimilar aspects as fashion, feelings, aesthetics, or aspirations. With Priscila I cater to the first and last of these requirements. When I go out with her (rarely, as you already know), I submit to fashion and to social aspirations. When I stay in with L, feelings and aesthetics prevail. With L, first I *see*, and I like and am excited by what I see. Sometimes I am first seized by excitement, and only later do I surrender, gratified, to the contemplation of L's beauty, tranquility, and beatific gaze, glowing with satisfaction.

The little savage inside me is thus tamed by the pleasure I experience with L. I believe that I also control the intimate beast when I live with Priscila in her father's house or when we—very, very rarely—attend some high-society event as a couple.

Judge me if you must. Perhaps I was inspired by the freedom of expression allowed to the liberated part of my being (which coexists with L). I might also have been spurred on by the political aspects of another side of that same liberated part of my being (which I use among my business associates—why did they greet me in sunglasses?). For whatever reason, at a seated dinner of twelve people, I reacted impulsively when Priscila, always inappropriate, took advantage of an angel's passing—an awkward silence at the table—to disturb the peace with a wind of her own.

That release of intestinal exhaust was a single wind in three distinct movements. Priscila first let out a thunderous fart, as if to attract attention, followed by the sound of a succession of bubbles, and ending with a—silent but deadly—gas that reached every nose and spoiled the red snapper that we had just been served. Priscila's odors were stronger than those of the capers, onions, tomatoes, and fish.

I broke the awkward silence that followed the fart attack by repeating aloud a secular mantra:

"Shut up, Priscila. You don't know what you're talking about."

The conversation resumed. Tom talked about the fluctuations of the exchange rate. His wife, about the rising costs of groceries. Dick said that he'd covered the Mexico City-Acapulco highway in record time—two hours and fifteen minutes—though nobody noticed and he was awarded no trophy. Mrs. Dick said she'd just returned from Houston with all the latest fashions you just can't find in Mexico. Harry complained about the price of gasoline, and Mrs. Harry about the vicissitudes of finding good domestic help.

That's how, among opinions about money earned and money spent, Priscila's unwelcome airs were dispelled. She didn't realize I had been responding to her, and answered my statement, "You don't know what you're talking about," with a lively, "Tomorrow is Sunday, a day of observance. Hooray!"

I wonder why I said what I said after my wife's olfactory and aural attack? To divert people's attention from Priscila's noticeable passing of gas in a way that would bring us back to the conversation initially interrupted by the proverbial passing of the angel?

My mantra was something of an unforgivable sequel, here and now, to my free and playful conversation with L, making use of the conversational style that I always save for our time together. I don't usually reveal in public, as I just had, my sense of humor. Likewise, as a reflection of my regular bureaucratic habit of bringing a situation to an end with a sentence that is at once abrupt, gracious, and indisputable, I said, "The sun rises every day."

Worse, saying "Shut up, Priscila. You don't know what you're talking about" was an inappropriate airing of my bad relationship with my wife. My unacceptable faux pas must have made me seem, at the very least, a rotten person to the Toms, Dicks, and Harrys. My exclamation, "Shut up. You don't know what you're talking about," implied a lack of necessary control over my wife and her explosions, and my own lack of discretion and self-control when the skies thundered, though (and only at the expense of poor Priscila) I had shown my presence of mind in covering up the situation and moving on to something else. As a result, I inspired admiration for my quickness, but also surprise that my reaction was a veiled chastisement of Priscila, known for flouting the law of cause and effect.

"Tomorrow is Sunday."

Because I don't accompany her to many dinners in society, I can't be certain if Priscila's flatulence is rare or part of her normal digestion at such events. How often has Priscila challenged the environmental purity of a dinner like this one without any reports reaching me? Do they hear her? Are her sonorities lost in the midst of animated conversation? Are they heard and ignored? Do people comment with sarcastic giggles, "Counseler Adam Gorozpe's wife is Queen of the Fart?"

Feeling, despite myself, like a latter-day Francisco de Quevedo y Villegas, I withdrew, complimenting myself on own ability to turn physical nastiness into literary reference.

For, back in the Golden Age of Spanish literature, in the seventeenth century, did not the great Quevedo write that the glory of the asshole is evident because it is "round like a sphere," and "its place is in the center, like that of the sun," and that "as it is such a necessary, precious, and beautiful thing, we keep it hidden away in the safest part of our body, protected between two soft walls . . . so that even light can't touch it," explaining "why we say: 'Kiss me where the sun don't shine,'" and adding "that joy reigns between the buttocks," especially in the case of "the fart . . . which is a merry thing, because whenever a fart is cut, laughter and joking ensue, bringing down the house," even if the other guests at the dinner table don't accept that thesis when they ignore Priscila's sonorities, forgetting (or ignoring) Quevedo and his pun: "Between a rock and a rock, the apricot booms."

I then evoked the aromas of a sliced lime with its juice dripping, fresh-cut grass, and a foamy cup of hot chocolate: smells that go directly to the pleasure centers, avoiding the obstacles of reason, smell as a reminder of emotion.

15

Where do all these people come from? I look at photos of them arranged on the tabletop, and I try to picture their *origins*, the only clue being their mansions, brand new or recently acquired from people who were until recently rich, mansions distorted by doors better suited for a prison, colored bunting, barricaded windows, men with concealed machine guns on the rooftops, gardeners who mow the lawn while looking around, on the alert, their overalls bulging with weapons.

Where do all the weapons come from? I receive a report. In Houston, Texas alone there are fifteen-hundred gun shops. A customer can purchase more than a hundred guns in one spree by touring dozens of legitimate stores willing to sell them, no questions asked. There are also gunrunners who smuggle contraband arms from the United States to Mexico. Buying rifles, shotguns, and handguns in the land of our northern neighbors does not require a license. Most of the pistols and rifles confiscated in Mexico come from stores and gun shows in Texas and Arizona.

The possession of guns—according to the report I read this morning—is legal in the United States, and if a suspicious shipment is detained between the store and the border, the trafficker is exercising, in any case, "the right of the people to keep and bear arms," established in the second amendment to the Constitution, part of the Bill of Rights, predicated on the existence of "A well regulated militia, being necessary to the security of a free State." I wonder how that well-regulated militia is working out.

An arms dealer, when questioned, responded that he didn't keep a record of what he had sold to someone else, and that he had sold his business. So how does he make a living now? "I live off my savings," he said from the porch of his mansion in Houston. "When were you audited before you retired?" "Well, they're allowed to audit you once a year, but there aren't enough auditors to go around, so sometimes every three years, or every six . . ." "What kinds of weapons did you sell?" "Guns, just guns." "What about AK-47 rifles?" "Achy whats? Doesn't ring a bell." "Maybe this'll ring a bell. We sent a plant to your store to buy twelve AK-47s, and you sold them to him. Didn't you think that was a suspicious request?" "The customer is always right. Listen, I'm just a simple retailer."

"I have the right to buy guns to go hunting. That's a Constitutional right."

"I have the right to sell guns. The Constitution . . ."

"I let the authorities know when there's a suspicious gun sale in my store. That's my professional obligation . . ."

"I don't say anything to anybody, because one word and the drug traffickers will . . ."

I receive reports about weapons confiscated in Mexico. A rifle in Acapulco was found after an attack on the offices of the Attorney General that left three secretaries dead. Two rifles confiscated on federal highways. A rifle found in Miahuatlán after an attack on army personnel at the local botanical garden.

I do the math.

Four weapons recovered by the authorities in Mexico. Four.

Thousands of guns imported by the drug cartels. Thousands.

Mansions with metal doors, colored bunting, barricaded windows, gunmen on the rooftops, armed gardeners.

"You can fit any number of things in a pair of overalls . . ."

Where did they come from? Who were they before? Can they be punished by being sent back to where they came from? By jailing or interrogating their women?

As so many times before, I take the bull by the horns and send undercover Jenaro Rubalcava, an accomplished cross-dresser doing time in the underground jail of San Juan de Aragón, to Santa Catita Prison to uncover information and, with luck, to get lucky. (I calculate the times that the distinguished Mr. Rubalcava has served in exchange for a reduction in his prison sentence.) Why don't I send a woman? Because I believe implicitly that women make up a fervent sisterhood that sticks together to defend itself from the intrusive, malevolent male, who on top of everything else, is a player if he can get away with it, and a bitch if he gives himself to another man.

The redeemed prisoner Rubalcava informs me that in Santa Catita there is an area dedicated to women drug traffickers, kidnappers, and serial killers. The Queen of Mambo is there, a busty and longhaired young woman who wears jeans, white sneakers, and a loose sweatshirt, as though to conceal her virtues. She manages Boss Big Snake's money on a computer in her cell, even though a guard accompanies her at all times. Pumped up, she walks around the prison courtyard, where about a hundred people are heaped together, including those who come in from the outside with food and clothing for the prisoners. There is Chachacha, accused of stabbing a banker: an attractive woman, in Rubalcava's estimation, whose low-cut blouse, combined with her tied-back hair, shows off the whiteness of her skin and distracts people from her cynical expression of satisfaction with her crime. Then there's Major Alberta, accused of kidnapping and murdering young millionaires. There are the two "dynamiters," accused of planting bombs willy-nilly throughout the capital. They are both cross-eyed and wear too much lipstick.

"The worst of them all, sir," says the very diligent Don Jenaro, "is a murderer of old ladies who has senselessly killed a dozen random little old ladies she stole nothing from. She kills for the joy of killing, and she argues that her victims were decrepit, already too prone to lying in bed, and are happier dead than alive.

"The most interesting inmate is Comandante Caramelo, a fat girl whose mouth is always stuffed with candy, who heads a group of criminal women who don't come, Mr. Gorozpe, from the lower depths of poverty. No, all of them were typists, bank employees, store clerks, nannies for rich kids, all women who were unsatisfied, not because of their poverty, but owing to the scarcity of their wealth, and wanting, Caramelo told me, to rise quickly in a society that promises everything but doesn't specify when that promise will be fulfilled.

"'We were in a hurry,' Caramelo said. 'We could have resigned ourselves to working in an office or in a pharmacy. But you know what, Counselor? What they promise us, others—a select few—already have, and they aren't going to let it go, and the life we're promised in ads, you know, we already know that's pure hope, and that we won't get any part of it, not even on the installment plan.'"

Caramelo brought another piece of caramel to her mouth. She dropped the wrapper on the floor. One of the dynamiters picked it up and carried it off to the trash can.

And then, "Are you surprised, sir, that we are making our own luck?" Caramelo had asked, stunning my envoy, Don Jenaro, whose disguise had been useless.

I admit that all of these reports leave me very dissatisfied. It is as if a thousand-headed hydra had stationed itself in front of my office on the fortieth floor overlooking Bosque de Chapultepec Park, and I bravely went out to cut off one of its heads only to see that two more heads had grown in its place.

We struggle against a polymorphous monster, and the solutions that I come up with—and that I present to my associates—are inadequate, temporary, or at best would only yield long-term benefits. To legalize drugs, a little at a time, beginning with marijuana. To know that the United States will not accompany us, even in the name of individual freedom, in allowing anyone to poison himself and others. To understand that this is a global problem in a global age: cut off two hydra heads and they are replaced by four heads . . .

My associates stare at me with skepticism from behind their black sunglasses. I *imagine* their stares anyway. Are they reproachful? Well then, they can propose something. One of them dares to speak up.

"Adam—"

"Hey now, don't get cheeky."

"No, not you, sir," he continues, "Adam *Góngora*."

"He's a murderer."

"And what else do criminals deserve, but a criminal who is more criminal than they are? With all due respect."

16

I have dinner with my brother-in-law Abelardo Holguín. He tells me about his disappointments in literary circles and of his opportunity to enter instead the world of television as a writer of soap operas.

He tells me about his conversation with the chief executive honcho of the Tetravision network, the elderly Rodrigo Pola, whom I have heard a lot about because his career was recorded in a prehistoric novel. Pola was the son of Rosenda Zubarán and Gervasio Pola, an officer of the Revolution executed by a firing squad in 1913 along with the comrades he snitched on so that he wouldn't die alone—"to die together" shouting "Viva Madero!" After all that, Rodrigo married Pimpinela de Ovando, an aristocrat whose family went back to the Porfirio Diaz dictatorship. (Does anybody remember those distant times?) He entered the new world of television, where he rose to become a chief executive officer, a powerful media business mogul.

Abelardo admits that he abused the privileges implicit in the name of his father in order to get to Don Rodrigo Pola. Pola didn't need to know that Abelardo was estranged from his famous father the King of Bakery any more than that he had been exiled from the republic of letters by the literary pope.

Luckily the magic surname Holguín opened doors to the young man, whose appearance, moreover, was already a calling card.

Abelardo Holguín had not given in to the youthful fashions that compel one to dress like a railroad worker or a beggar; rather, an enthusiast of Hollywood films from the thirties and forties, he dressed conservatively, with a jacket and tie, like Cary Grant. Abelardo and I had in common this love for old movies and that lost era, which survives only on film. Sometimes Priscila used to walk in on our conversations, which she suspected were conducted in some sort of code:

"Thomas Mitchell, in the year 1939 alone," Abelardo reminded me, "appears in *Only Angels Have Wings*, *Gone With The Wind*, *The Hunchback of Notre Dame*, *Mr. Smith Goes to Washington*, and *Stagecoach*, for which he won the Oscar for best supporting actor."

"*Stagecoach*," I said, picking up the thread, "is an adaptation of *Boule de Suif*, the short story by Maupassant, and Norman Foster brought it to the screen in Mexico with Esther Fernández and Ricardo Montalbán."

"Who was Foster's wife's brother-in-law: they were both married to Blaine sisters, the most famous of which was Loretta Young."

"Who had a secret lovechild with Clark Gable, conceived during the shooting of *The Call of the Wild*, based on the Jack London novel—"

"Which enjoyed many screen adaptations, notably *The Sea Wolf* with John Garfield and Ida Lupino."

"And the rest of that cast. That actor, you know, that one who was introduced with such pomp and circumstance. What was his name? And then he just disappeared."

"I don't remember. Ask Carlos Monsiváis."

"Or José Luis Cuevas."

"Or as a last and best resort, Natalio Botana."

That Priscila had been eavesdropping on us from the dining room next door, hidden behind a curtain, became apparent when Don Celestino stormed in to reproach Abelardo, as usual, and me as well, which was less usual.

"What are you and your brother-in-law secretly discussing in the living room?"

"It's no secret. They're classic movies."

"Movies?" Don Celes becomes agitated. "Did you say moo-vies? A secret code made from movies, I reckon. So what are you and Adam whispering about? What are you up to? What are you plotting against your sister? And who is this Norman Foster character anyway?"

I hear the slap that Priscila, upon hearing these words, unleashes on the maid who is taking clean laundry up to the bedroom.

"Father, Norman Foster is a film director."

"Sure. A di-rec-tor, huh? That's all you're going to fess up to?"

"He directed *Journey into Fear.*"

"Okay, now the cat's out of the bag. So that's the password. Journey into fear?"

"Starring Dolores del Río—"

"Don't change the subject, rascal, scoundrel."

I find it amusing that old-man Holguín uses the same expressions as the old lady who beat up that youthful mugger with an umbrella on the Salto-del-Agua-to-Ciudadela-to-Rayón bus.

"Congratulations," I tell Abelardo with a laugh, now that we are having lunch at El Danubio on República de Uruguay Street. "You've freed yourself from Don Celestino."

"But you're still there," Abelardo said without malice.

"There is nothing quite like being seen to render a person invisible," I said with a smile.

Don Rodrigo Pola, who must almost be a centenarian, received Abelardo Holguín, as I said, in his sacrosanct office on Insurgentes, stuffed inside what seemed to be a wicker basket full of cotton that supposedly conserves his energies and provides him with the warmth that he lacks or returns his warmth and energy to him, in essence poisoning himself. How much heat does an almost hundred-year-old crow generate? That's not just a physical question, but a philosophical one: why are there people who survive beyond the "normal" life span—seventy or eighty years?—losing, true, many faculties, but maintaining or perhaps gaining other, previously unknown ones? It's sad to see men who were vigorous, quarrelsome, even fighters, reduced to muteness and the wheelchair, depending on the wives whom they mistreated, cheated on, and despised throughout their marriages, to help them eat, piss, sleep, and to wheel them back and forth. Wouldn't it be preferable to die rather than to be so thoroughly humiliated?

I tell myself—and I don't tell Abelardo—that I would rather die while I still have the full use of my faculties and am still strong and active, before I'm ever subjected to forgetfulness or pity, or cause sorrow to this young man visiting the old coot whom he once admired and who served as his role model, now reduced to drooling and speaking nonsense from a wicker basket . . .

Perhaps for all of these reasons, Don Rodrigo Pola, who's still sharp as a tack, has not given in to the usual supports required by old age—wheelchair, crutches, the sickbed itself—but has opted to station himself inside a wicker basket lined with cotton.

That's how he greets Abelardo, giving him a passive but eloquent welcome from that cottony throne where he preserves and recovers the strength that remains with an elegant gesture of resignation and a sort of performance—Abelardo believes—for which he has mustered all the strength of his advanced age and physical weakness to conjure an atmosphere of imperial twilight.

"Like the High Lama in *Lost Horizon*."

"Played by Sam Jaffe."

"And directed by Frank Capra."

"Dad, Daddy," Priscila would say, "Abelardo and Adam are speaking in code. They've got something up their sleeves. It must be a plot against me. Expose them, Daddy, defend your daughter. Twelve o'clock and all is well." And then she'd slap the maid in the face.

What kind of conspiracy would she imagine if she heard the media czar, old man Rodrigo Pola, talking to young Abelardo Holguín, explaining to him the secrets of soap operas?

Pola addresses Abelardo ceremoniously as "sir." He doesn't call him "young man," "kid," or even "Abelardo," but "sir," establishing right away a respectful relationship, appropriate for work. As Abelardo explained to me, Pola is saying, I greet you as you are, Holguín, son of the King of Bakery, but don't think that being part of an illustrious family gives you power beyond just being greeted by me here in the upper echelons of our television station. Then Pola thinks again, Abelardo tells me, and says, "Perhaps your membership in Mexico's circle of privilege counts for something. You are part of the one hundred, two hundred families that *count*, that share the businesses, the financial and political jobs, the invitations to weddings, dinners, vacations, and so on. Isn't that enough? Then wake up sir, and realize that we are being threatened."

Perhaps at this moment Don Rodrigo Pola sighs, and Abelardo becomes alarmed thinking that each of the old man's hiccups could be his *last*. But he speaks again, to Abelardo's youthful admiration, when Abelardo asks, "Threatened?"

Don Rodrigo looks to the right and the left with suspicion, half-submerged in cotton.

"Look, sir, you have to realize something. My father was a revolutionary in 1910. I was born in 1909. I was left alone with my mother, *Doña* Rosenda, may she rest in peace. I wanted to be a writer. After a while, I became disillusioned. I dedicated myself to what was coming, not what had gone before. That is your task, sir. To understand what it is that remains and not what has gone before. When a country goes broke and its elite disappear, another country emerges in its place, and in this new country, it's hard to tell who the new elite is. President Madero was the son of landowners, Carranza had been a senator during the Porfirio Díaz administration. But Obregón was a farmer, Calles a teacher, and well, Villa and Zapata, imagine . . ."

Did Rodrigo Pola sigh while telling you, Abelardo, what you already knew?

"But all of them were *political* men, the intellectuals as well as the ignoramuses. In other words, they wanted *power* in order to transform the country. And they did it. A modern, industrial society was created, sure, one with way too much social backwardness, a backwardness that for better or for worse we have tried to amend. But now, my dear sir, Abelardo Holguín . . ."

Don Rodrigo widened his big eyes from within his cotton shroud.

"Now it is not the revolutionaries who are coming. The ones who are coming are the criminals, the drug traffickers, the whores who accompany them, the bodyguards, and as usual, the government officials with Swiss bank accounts of unknown origin.

"An entire race of vicious people, people of an inconceivable vulgarity, sir, people without class. They're not townspeople, nor middle class, nor any class. They are the underclass, *lumpen*, empowered by crime. They are the kidnappers of society, the most sinister, cruel, and voracious social climbers, without any ideals, ready to murder, exploit, corrupt . . ."

He sighed one last time.

"Are we going to fight back with soap operas?"

Abelardo says that the old man smiled. It was hard to be sure, as he was underneath a lot of cotton.

"Well, yes, sir. We are going to gamble on the fact that a lot of people are going to attach themselves to their television sets instead of going out into the streets to pursue a career in crime. And even in the homes of the criminals, who knows if one of our dramas will touch one or two little hearts and show them the path to virtue?"

This time the smile was sour. Pola cleared his throat (everything about him seemed final, blunt), and he sat up as best as he was able to inside the basket.

"You told me you want to be a writer? Well you can choose. There are different styles of soap operas. The worst are the Venezuelan shows. They're full of people with too many names. Half of the running time is taken up with them calling each other Francisco Edelmiro Bolívar or Edelmira Scarlett Miroslava, and nothing happens because they're all too busy saying their long names. The Brazilian ones are the best, though not in a style available to us. Too much politics. Too much nudity. Too much hanky-panky. In Colombian soaps, however, a kind of national prudery exists despite the intrusion of crime and drugs."

Abelardo expressed, he tells me, anticipation.

"In Mexico, my dear sir, Don Abelardo Holguín, we won't admit a single controversial theme in our soap operas. There are the good guys and the bad guys. There are powerful and evil men. There are manipulative women. There are families with mixed children, good and bad. But there is—it is indispensable—the modest and honorable little maid with whom the well-to-do boy, the baby of the family, falls in love."

Abelardo said he did not recognize the noise that emerged from the basket. Was it the laughter of old man Rodrigo Pola? Or his particular way of expiring?

"Don't go beyond those parameters, sir. Everything is encoded in that discourse: country, family, religion, and state."

"And the ending?" asked Abelardo.

"The maid marries the well-to-do boy."

"And the inheritance?" he thought to ask.

"First he loses it," Pola said, shifting around in his pre-deathbed.

"But then the hero makes another fortune, this time by his own hard work and individual initiative. He doesn't inherit it, and he doesn't lose the girl he chose from the servile cattery."

Abelardo says that the old man, upon saying this, sucked on his own gums, making the sound of a death rattle.

"Anyway," he said to Abelardo, "let's have a toast to the success of your work. Pour yourself a glass of wine. Drink. I can assure you that this wine has never seen the light of day."

17

Up until this point of my life I have woven together the different threads of my existence with great skill. As I have explained, I lead my professional life with extreme seriousness, with no tolerance for frivolity or misbehavior on the part of my associates. My family life disguises my professional life. In Don Celestino Holguín's home, I act like what I originally was: the poor kid who hit the jackpot with Priscila, Princess of the Carnival. But both disguises—professional and family—conceal, at the same time, my erotic life, my passionate surrender to L, with whom the hours of nuisance, formality, presumptuousness, and absence turn into moments of communication, freedom, naturalness, and presence.

L's person, love, and company are so important to me. But does L realize how important? I have to admit that I don't know. I don't know because I also don't really know *who* L is.

One could think of L as a frivolous being, diaphanous, a bird that flits around the garden from flower to flower sipping nectar. L gets excited at a Luismi concert and asks me to do such frivolous things as shaving my armpits, and does this, that, and the other.

But I've never seen anyone display such seriousness in everyday behavior. I have never seen an apartment better arranged than L's. Everything is in its exact place, as if by magic. Sex unleashes chaos on beds, bathrooms, closets; nobody thinks twice about leaving underwear, shirts, and socks where they lie, evidence of passion, of erotic haste. Like the gnomes in fables, however, L has everything back in its place quicker than a cock can crow—quicker at least than I can enter the bathroom, shower, and return to the bedroom, at which time the room looks as though nothing had happened there. L is already dressed and waits for me in the living room, offering to make a cocktail for me. As though the scotch and soda were a prize for my small tour de force of lovemaking.

L knows that I'm an ambitious man. Everybody knows a lot about me from the newspapers, but L never asks me anything. I sometimes suffer a bit from that tacit barrier that L imposes: we come here to love each other, to be together, to fantasize. "If you want, Adam," L says, "I can tell you what I do. I know what you do, and I don't need any explanations: love me, I don't ask for anything else; love me, Adam . . ." I mention this about L because this afternoon, I don't know for what reason, I feel compelled to say something about myself that I've never brought up before, though it's something everybody already knows:

"I'm an ambitious man."

L looks at me with "distance"—an affectionate distance, but distance nonetheless. L gathers ice cubes from the freezer and makes the usual sound by transferring them to a cut glass container, as if to disguise any importance that I may want to attribute to the conversation. I am grateful for this tone of normality. L brings me the glass of scotch and sits, smiling at my side.

L drinks an Orange Crush and listens to me with the distance between a scotch-on-the-rocks and an Orange Crush.

"I'm an ambitious man," I repeat.

L catches my drift. "They say, Adam, that you've achieved everything that you set out to do."

"I'm an ambitious man."

"You've said so three times. Why?"

"Why do you think? "

"Okay. You have accomplished your previous ambitions. Now you have a new ambition. You're a regenerated man. You're Adam, the first man . . ."

L caresses my hand for just an instant.

"What for?" L asks.

"You said it." I return L's caress and realize that my fingers have retained the cold of the glass of whisky that I'd placed on the table.

"No, I mean, what are you ambitious for? Why are you ambitious about whatever you're ambitious for?"

The reader will understand that I can talk to L about everything and nothing, about the greatest and the smallest things, without fear of reprisals, misinterpretation, or any lies. And yet, I wonder whether this evening, which is unexpectedly upon us, I am authorized to speak even more openly, and whether my words, more than anything else, have been dictated by the dust storm that eclipsed the sun and darkened my large office windows at noon.

I dive into the trust that L gives me, counting on the temperature of that welcoming soul, which to me is a liquid thing, something fluid that contrasts with the stagnant waters of my family and professional life. L is water that flows tranquil and clear.

I can admit, just like that, that I feel threatened. My life has reached a kind of plain on which satisfaction prevails over the rest of my ambition, making my ambition feel tamed, like a tiger that once roamed the jungle freely, stalking its enemies, defeating the weak and, more importantly, subjugating the strong, but that has now accepted the rules of domestic peace, the cage in which he can both pace and remain still, eat without the risk of being eaten, sleep soundly, and observe the world from the heights of a voluntary prison because his own power is locked up in there, a domestic beast that I, Adam Gorozpe, can feed, dominate like any fluffy old fur ball or set free to roam the city, inflicting panic and sometimes sowing death . . .

L expresses sympathy, resisting any impulse to put certainty into words: *I know that.* The very gradual change in L's look implies a *now what?* And is there something that has shaken your confidence, Adam? Have they weighed down your wings, baby, are you flying lower today than you flew yesterday?

I say that, as we both know, I've always described my private life, my career, and the society in which I live, as a paradoxical cage of freedom. I am free because my life is what I am, caged, yes, because all human society is a cage, but a cage dominated by Adam Gorozpe, do you understand?

"I don't deny the limits of my freedom. I endure them because I have more power than freedom, do you understand me? Do you believe me?"

As in the opera by Puccini set in a bohemian garret, L says, very softly, "Yes."

L would never demand an explanation, and I admit that it is hard for me to give one. A doubt gnaws at me: does L deserve anything less than my total honesty? At what point is being honest with a lover supplying ammunition for a future firing squad? Is being honest with the person who now, at this moment, conjugates and captures my passion, also giving this lover weapons to use for revenge when we are no longer lovers?

The reader will understand that my other sexual relationship, with Priscila, already proceeds with established, unbreakable rules of conduct. She is who she is and does what she does: everything is foreseeable as confirmed by twenty-one years of living together. Nothing changes in Priscila and my marriage. I never demand change or, God forbid, a divorce. Priscila is my continuity, my permanence, and if she doesn't give me great joy, at least she does give me security and peace. In that sphere, things are the way they are. Priscila says stupid things. Don Celes hollers. Abelardo leaves home. The maid gets a slap.

Here, with L, my soul is satisfied, though satisfaction itself might presage dissatisfaction in that today's sweetness includes the promise of unforeseen bitterness. That's the great erotic toss-up: if you give it all to me today, can you take it all away from me tomorrow? We feel free from the matrimonial knot that becomes a noose around the condemned man's neck. And we feel threatened because, without the legal commitment, freedom, because it is free, can free itself from all obligations, leaving one lover abandoned on a solitary island with no company other than regrets, the twisted ordeals of jealousy, nostalgia, all the debts of love's sadness . . .

What about divorce? Separation? Neither of these matters to a couple who desire each other and who satisfy their desire. Nothing else matters. And nothing else matters because passion covers all the spaces of existence. Passion leaves no window, door, or hole through which to escape. Is sincerity a virtue or is it the condition of erotic terror and ardor? This is what I need to find out with L, despite many reservations, fears, and surprising audacities, on this twilight evening darkened by the dust storms of the city's dry season.

December seems so very far away!

18

"Nobody better try to take my place. Don't even think about it."

"'Don't even think about it?' He knows everything."

"Even what I'm thinking to myself?"

"Everything, I'm telling you, the guy's a mind reader."

"Isn't loyalty enough?"

"No no no, not at all. The more loyal you are, the more expendable you're gonna be. Or, I don't know, less trustworthy or something."

"So, how is that different from being with the opposition?"

"Not so very different. But if you're with the opposition, you're safer than if you're a collaborator."

"So, loyalty isn't enough?"

"It's just better to sacrifice people who are loyal than for the leader to sacrifice himself or be sacrificed by them. The supreme ruler can't tolerate anybody surpassing him. Nobody is allowed to go off on his own."

"What happened with Largo?"

"They locked him up. Then they paid him a visit in jail and said, 'If you confess, you can save yourself.' He confessed, and they put him in front of a firing squad."

"Where did they bury him?"

"In an unmarked grave."

"But he was part of our history; he deserves to be remembered . . ."

"He was exiled from history."

"And Bobby, what happened to Bobby?"

"They took away his privileges. He confessed his errors."

"Did they shoot him, too?"

"Nope, these days he's a gondolier in Xochimilco. He's on what they call 'the pajama plan.' Instead of executing you, they turn you into a gardener, a chauffeur, a . . ."

"A gondolier in Xochimilco."

"'Nobody better try to take my place.' That's clear."

"But he's about to turn ninety-nine."

"'Don't even think about it—'"

"Don't even don't even don't even . . ."

"Think about it think about it think about it . . ."

"Adam Gorozpe is the ruler of Mexico for life."

I woke up with a start unable to breathe. I touched my forehead. A nightmare.

19

No, that wasn't a nightmare. It was real. Adam Góngora has been put in charge of public security—or what little remains of it—and has already demonstrated his tactics.

"We are all all-but corpses," was his first, macabre statement to the press.

You wouldn't know that by looking at him! Góngora is a chubby and squat little man with a face like cooked ham and a borrowed haircut combed over his bald spot. His hat makes him a few centimeters taller. He refuses, however, to wear cuban heels. He is proud that despite his short stature, he has attained the heights of power. He has been appointed to impose a semblance of order in the growing chaos of the republic.

He makes provocative statements:

"We all know that our national security is pretty insecure. The forces of order ally themselves easily with the forces of disorder. The police earn miserable salaries. The criminals increase officers' salaries from three thousand pesos a month to three hundred thousand. How do you like that? The army is called in to perform work unsuitable to the armed forces. The army is now devoted to police work, and it is defeated by criminals who are better armed than it is. How do you like that?"

And here is Góngora's solution:

"I will purge the forces of law and order. There will be fewer, but better paid, police officers. Let's see if that way . . . how do you like that?"

Let's see. "We are all all-but corpses. How do you like that?"

Góngora's new position as chief of public security allows him to enter the highest strata of society. He receives invitations. He accepts them. Everyone wants Góngora's protection. Even my father-in-law, the King of Bakery, throws a dinner for the diminutive policeman.

"Put some cushions on the chair so that he can reach his soup," I tell my father-in-law, who is not unaware of my negative opinion of Góngora.

"Oh, this little Adam is such a little joker," jokes the King.

Time to move the story along. There's no point beating around the bush, given all that's happened. Now you have a portrait of Adam Góngora. Now you know that he is, unfortunately, my namesake. And to make matters worse, at dinner, when people say Adam, we don't know if they mean Adam Gorozpe—me—or Adam Góngora—him.

All this is just a prelude. The curtain rises and my eyes see, and my senses register, something astonishing. Góngora won't stop talking. He knows that he's new and in demand. He knows that he's the star. Maybe he is intelligent enough to realize that once their novelty wears off, the stars die, and then nobody looks at them. He is obviously unschooled. But he is also suspicious and cunning because he suspects other people of being cunning. He is aware that whatever he says tonight he can't repeat on some other occasion, because, first, everybody will know what he is going to say, and second, because they will be bored to death.

I watch him prattle, as he tries to surprise and tries to frighten the guests seated around Don Celes's table. If he's smart, he won't accept another dinner invitation at this house. Adam Góngora is one of those men who, at the first opportunity, give away everything they have or know how to give. Socially, they die with one shot. But they don't know it, and when they appear again, they inspire yawns and invite ridicule. This offends them deeply so they respond with cruelty. They run out of words. They are left with action: resentful action, punitive action.

I realize all this when I observe Góngora's behavior at the dinner that my father-in-law gives for him. But this—so predictable of someone entering new spheres of power—is not what captures my attention. There is something that I wouldn't have predicted.

Priscila can't take her eyes off of Góngora. And Góngora in turn, no matter how much he babbles on, constantly addresses Priscila, stares at her, *exalts* her. I know my wife all too well. She became accustomed to everybody's attention in the days when she was the Queen of Spring and the Princess of the Carnival. Ever since she married me, she no longer feared adding kilos on fad diets and pages to her calendar. But she felt a loss because no one ever wooed her again.

As you know, nothing that Priscila does bothers me. Her complacence is, in fact, part of my life's master plan. Hard-nosed lawyer. Conventional husband. Ardent lover. The office. Priscila. L. These are my discursive laws.

And now this intruder comes to disrupt the careful order of my life. This busybody, who is also my namesake, stares at Priscila with growing ardor until my wife blushes, lowers her eyes, then opens them for Mr. Góngora. She lets herself be loved.

I do something inappropriate.

Something shameful.

I let my napkin fall. I bend down to pick it up.

I watch what is happening under the table.

I can't believe this.

My Priscila and he, Góngora, are playing footsie. They touch the tips of their feet. Priscila takes off a pink shoe, Góngora (with more difficulty) an ankle boot, and both rejoice in this secret meeting of limbs, this prelude of intimacy to come.

The picture I have of my life changes at that very moment and suggests unaccustomed enigmas and challenges in areas that I'd believed would remain forever ordered.

20

The next things I discreetly observe are Góngora's policies intended to reestablish order.

Góngora lays waste to the camps known, to my injury and insult, as *Gorozpevilles*, all the while blaming the business sector for the poverty and marginalization of these beings he detains, imprisons, and abuses, accusing them of being bums, delinquents, and social blights, when everybody knows that most of them are middle- or lower-middle-class people who lost their jobs, savings, and apartments and had nowhere else to go but to the lost cities, the shanty towns on the outskirts of the capital.

Jobs and savings. Also homes, houses in nice neighborhoods, on which, from one day to the next, they could no longer keep up mortgage payments. Able people who lacked only foresight, reduced to the misery that always surrounds Mexico's islets of relative prosperity.

Large numbers of seasonal field laborers, migrant workers who no longer have a way out of the country, have also ended up in the *Gorozpevilles*—I've had it up to here with that offensive little name! Since the northern border was sealed, the migrants have had no choice but to camp here, without jobs, and more devastatingly still, without official work programs, all abolished because as we exist in a market economy, we trust the market to solve the problem of labor supply and demand. *Yeah sure!* I think, disappointed by the very theory that I helped make official: the State is bad, the market is good, the State is an ogre, the market is a fairy godmother . . .

These are the camps where the forces of order led by Adam Góngora come to unleash attack dogs, to burn down miserable shacks, to rip the stuffing out of mattresses and sofas, and to tighten the garrote on whoever refuses to abandon their piece of turf, and because they can't be too careful, on those who don't refuse. I wonder if the denizens had only come to the misnamed *Gorozpevilles* because they were forced to abandon their homes in Anzures and Patriotismo. Where can they possibly go from here? What is left for them? The mountains? The volcanoes? The open countryside? Cuernavaca? Toluca? That's a mystery. We'll see. Perhaps Góngora has a master plan I could only imagine: could my sinister namesake be some sort of a demographer with a plan to decongest Mexico City by culling some of its excess population and forcing those people to migrate to the provinces?

Please observe what a good person I am. I give Góngora the benefit of the doubt. I force myself to think so for the sake of the country. But this is a fleeting hope, an illusion of which I am soon disabused.

The repression is worse every day as it extends from the tents raised at the edges of the railway tracks to those people who find work in fairs and circuses—clowns, acrobats, horseback riders, midgets, and vendors of roasted pumpkin seeds, Pueblan sweet-potato desserts, or Zamoran sweet curdled-milk-with-cinnamon. What did they do to deserve this? Maybe nothing, but Góngora is fighting Tyrians and Trojans. He has to show his *strength* and that is easier to do by taking on *the weak* than *the criminal*. When will he dare take on *the powerful*? Ha!

He rounds up drug addicts, the criminally insane, the destitute, the drunks, hookers of all genders, people who have done nothing terrible but are identified (by Góngora) as blight. And I wonder, how far is he willing to go? And I answer my question with another question: why doesn't he pursue the culprits instead of just their victims? And I answer that question with yet another question: when will my turn come? When will Góngora come after me for A) being rich, and B) being married to Priscila?

Clause A becomes more immediate as Góngora increases his acts of violence, first against the poor, then against the impoverished, and finally against the rich. Of course these staggered measures depend on the public's approval, motivated more by resentment than by justice. Góngora finds culprits where there are only victims, but he doesn't shy away from punishing the rich, and this posture will win him more fans than if he had captured Al Capone red handed. I see Góngora come and go, small and intrusive, borrowed haircut, in the papers and on the news, and what is worse, in my own house, which belongs to my father-in-law Don Celestino Holguín, and where Góngora comes to "take tea" with the famous one-time Queen of the Veracruz Carnival, otherwise known as my wife.

All of which leads me to clause B and the renewed circumstances of my wife, Doña Priscila. At first, the *capo* Góngora comes over to have tea at the King of Bakery's house, but soon he doesn't have to come over because Priscila is stepping out. Where does she go? She leaves word that she is with her cousin Sonsoles, which is easy to confirm.

"No, Adam, Priscila isn't over here. I haven't seen her in months. See you, Adam. Bye."

This lack of discretion on Priscila's part only serves to confirm that the Queen of Carnival lies more than King Momo himself, and that she doesn't take precautions because she (so pious!) is not used to the deceit that I (so graceful!) practice with refined cunning.

I ask myself, my macho self, if there is any comparison between the taking of my wife and the taking of power. For most men, conquering a woman is proof enough of our manhood, and after the conquest, relaxed, we can return to our various occupations. For some men, worthy of compassion, the taking of power is victory enough, and they no longer need anything else: the woman is expendable, a housewife, an apron without a face. For others—and I think Góngora falls into this awful category—to have power and to have an "old lady" are equivalent and complementary. I understand, gentlemen, because that is my category as well. I have power, and I have a lover, and so help me God, ask me no more questions!

The most surprising thing, nevertheless, is the change that Góngora's attention has brought about in Priscila, a woman I thought I knew like the back of my hand, but who now turns out to be a fistful of ants that I can't control. What has happened? I don't want to entertain those most banal of all banalities: Priscila had sexual urges that I didn't know existed, much less how to satisfy; she adapted to our way of living because, like most women, she let herself be influenced. Comfort, husband, house, maids. It's difficult to imagine Priscila in another role, for example, that of Chachacha locked away in Santa Catita women's prison. Chachacha, however, seems like a nun compared to my wife, with the madness I suspect her of, and the Queen of Mambo is more faithful to the gangster Big Snake than the Queen of Spring is to me.

21

None of which is enough to interrupt the carnival of life:

M.A.M. (The Moral Alliance of Mexico) steps up its campaign against homosexuals. Families organize themselves against gays, even, and especially, against their own gay children. Upright parents demonstrate their moral courage. The brave paterfamilias of a house with a homosexual child hangs on his door the sign:

A PERVERT LIVES HERE

Pervert and *perversion* are M.A.M.'s favorite words. Their famous advice is to

TAKE CARE OF YOUR CHILDREN!

They have, indeed, organized themselves to an astonishing degree. In an interview with this newspaper, a young man who calls himself "Orchid" discussed the "precarious state" that has been his life since he came out of the closet. "My friends disappear then turn up dead," he complained. "I'm too afraid to leave my house, even though my dad says he'd rather have a dead son than a faggot one." Orchid clarifies: "But he doesn't mean it. He lets me stay in his house because, he says, on the streets I'd wind up dead. I tell him, 'I don't mind staying home. It's better to be gay than dead.'"

In Mexico City, the vast number of houses and apartments abandoned by occupants who have defaulted on their mortgages has inspired a new business (scare) tactic. The competition among real estate agents has become so fierce that they've had to launch smear campaigns against each other. Here are some recent ads:

- "Stop by the property on offer at Acatempan Street in the Famsa section. If this house doesn't scare you, you're probably already dead."

- "On Masaryk Avenue, the advertised house looks like an African bordello."

- "If you have a sense of humor, stop by the apartment for rent in Vallejo. You'll die laughing."

- "Don't be fooled. The property for sale in Eje South is located right off the municipal garbage dump. That's why it stinks!"

- "Are you a masochist? Then the house for sale at Virrey de la Cerda is perfect for you."

- "The apartment for rent at the Calzada San Joaquín has closets full of cockroach caca. Careful!"

- "Nostalgic for the days when people lived in caves? Then hurry over to the house in the hellishly misnamed Heaven's Corner before Trimalchio finds another caveman to rent it to first."

- "If you want to know what you're getting yourself into, pay a clandestine visit to the foyer of the building on the corner of Zarco and Valerio Trujano. Let us know how far you trust the creepy husband-and-wife porters."

- "If you want to know what it feels like to be spied on by your neighbors, spend the longest day of your life in the bedroom of the apartment for rent at Popocatéptl Plaza."

- "Like a nice dungeon? Then don't pass up the opportunity to rent the dank basement being passed off as a luxury apartment in Pushkin Gardens."

A forty-something-year-old woman showed up at our editorial office claiming to be the mother of the Boy-God who preaches on the corner of Insurgentes and Quintana Roo. When our reporter asked her whether she was the Virgin Mary, she answered emphatically that yes, she was. An examination performed by one of our in-house nurses disproved that latter claim.

Don Adam Góngora, chief of national security, released a much-discussed statement, announcing his deep nostalgia for the long period of rule by the Party of Revolutionary Institutions (PRI), when the unions belonged to the government, the right to strike was mythic, the workers were subject to the bossman, and the bossman was pro-government. Mister Góngora stressed that he was speaking out of nostalgia for simpler times and that he realized the past could not be repeated. Today, he explained, a different situation requires innovative measures. The most critical columnists have seen in these statements an intention to increase security, taking advantage of the nostalgia for a rotten past to prevent the horror of an even worse present.

The Sunday Boy-God has complained in no uncertain terms against the usurper who calls himself Jenaro González and asks that from now on the identity of his many imitators be challenged by demanding they show a particular birthmark that the Holy-Boy alone possesses. The Boy abstained from revealing information about this mark for fear that his imitators would tattoo themselves with counterfeits. Could it be on his little bottom? Just asking.

A well-known astrophysicist from the National Autonomous University of México, who asked to remain anonymous, considers that the comet many citizens saw last night isn't a comet at all, but a simple shift in the position of our sky in relation to the fixed stars. The scholar explained that this phenomenon is called "parallax," and that the word describes, for instance, the apparent shift of a planet's position as observed from two different points of view.

A prelate who asked to remain anonymous swiftly responded to the above statement, reminding us that in 1531 Halley's comet appeared in the sky on the same day that The Virgin of Guadalupe appeared to Juan Diego. Therefore we must not rule out religious truth, concluded the prelate, when faced with scientific superstition. Asked about the religious significance of yesterday's comet, the man of the Church said that to know this, we would need to know what we still don't know, but which will one day be revealed. The community of the faithful received this statement with applause.

Because of the profusion of Chinese tourists in Mexico, our waiters must learn Mandarin instead of—as in the old days—English. The Asian traveler also demands private dining rooms, which forces our restaurateurs to subdivide their spacious premises, once the pride of the food industry, with partitions, screens, and new walls. "The customer gets what the customer wants," explained the manager of the famous Bellinghausen restaurant in the famous Zona Rosa neighborhood.

Many professionals have abandoned their occupations, creating a dangerous shortage of doctors, lawyers, engineers, and architects. Asked about it, the interested parties responded, as if they had all agreed beforehand, "We are now freelancers." An inquisitive and suspicious journalist asked them if that meant they were *freeloaders*. Outraged, the group spokesman (for they have grouped together and selected a spokesman) replied: "All we want is to be our own bosses." (The mystery remains unsolved.)

M.A.M. (The Moral Alliance of Mexico) leaders held a press conference to announce their new national campaign to combat homosexuality. "This country doesn't need beggars or faggots," announced the M.A.M. president. "Let's purify the nation," he added, conceding that identifiable homosexuals, depending on the gravity of their misconduct, could be robbed, kidnapped, or killed. A furious father complained that his gay son decided to call himself "Angela" instead of "Angel" and proceeded to change his birth certificate, school diplomas, and passport, creating infinite confusion in dealing with the red tape of national bureaucracy. "What if all the pansies go change their names and need new identity documents?" asked the outraged father. The president of M.A.M. concluded with the statement: "We must all remember that Mexico is a religious, conservative, *violent, and very macho country* . . ." The furious crusader for chastity had nothing else to add, save, "Castrate them all."

22

I observe Góngora's movements. I don't let on that I know about his apparent affair with my poor wife, nor do I publicly declare myself opposed to his violent and arbitrary security measures.

I observe him and bide my time.

I know he'll seek me out: he seeks me out.

I don't know what he wants: he wants something. His attitude is a little smug. And more than a little threatening.

With courtesy and an undaunted face, I meet him in my office.

It's harder to look neutral, however, when Góngora approaches me with the treacherous intention of hugging me. As the reader knows (and if the reader doesn't, he or she is about to learn that), in Mexico a male hug is an essential rite of friendship, and Góngora doesn't want to miss out on that. But my deepest instincts warn me to reject him, not so much because I don't want to touch this guy—after all, politeness forces me to accept his hug—but because I suspect that Adam Góngora suffers from an advanced case of halitosis. A stench of malodorous indigestion precedes him, as if this poor devil who talks out of his ass also shits through his mouth. I find him suspicious. He approaches with the smells of street-fair corn, thick and nauseating shots of pulque, a foul burp, a dirty rag on his tongue, and a rotting animal on his gums.

But how am I going to avoid him?

I can't. I give in to politeness. My suspicions are confirmed. Adam Góngora *stinks*. He seems to flaunt his smell of intestinal corruption. His presence fills me with horror and doubt. How can my wife Priscila, who may be a fool but is at least a clean fool, stand such a stench? And the doubt. Is Góngora aware of his stench, and does he cultivate it as another aspect of his power? *Come on, let's see if you're man enough to get close to me without holding your nose. And by the way, your health and life depend on it, you miserable excuse for a worm.*

We embrace then, and I take all the precautions that the reader might imagine.

Anything to get to the point.

"What brings you here today?"

"Look, Gorozpe, my work in security entails responsibilities that are sometimes unpleasant, although necessary. I'm not trying to trick you . . ."

"Oh."

"For example, friendship. *How do you like that?*"

"Oh, of course."

"I try to avoid mixing my responsibilities and my friendships in the same sandwich. How do you like that?"

I smile. "Onions over here, tomatoes over there"—Góngora doesn't laugh—"but once you attain power . . ." He cracks a smile at that last word.

"Power? Don't you believe it. Power . . . Come on . . . ! Power . . . Don't kid yourself."

He cuts me off: "Power imposes responsibilities that are not the least bit pleasant, you know? How do you like that?"

"I know, I know. Wouldn't that be the sort of thing I'd know?"

"For instance, yesterday's friend is still today's friend, but . . ."

"But what . . . ? C'mon, tell me . . ."

"Now I know things about yesterday's friend that I didn't know about today's friend. How do you like that?"

"Such as?"

"Whoa now, don't make me get ahead of myself."

"Señor Góngora, you are my guest. I wouldn't make you do anything."

"Well there you go. Just yesterday, I was a private citizen with a good reputation . . . How do you like that?"

I abstain from smiling.

"Even if my enemies don't believe me."

"What about your friends?"

"Counselor, are you my friend?"

"I'm not your enemy, if that is what's worrying you."

"No, I'm asking are you my friend?"

"I wouldn't aspire to so much." I smile again, and pray the Lord not wipe away my smile, because that would give my interlocutor great pleasure.

He moves his lips in a creepy way. "So, it would only be halfway, so, so—"

"You know that a man like me deals with a lot of people. With courtesy, when they deserve it; rarely with friendship."

"And with disrespect?"

"Never, never. I was brought up right, know what I mean?"

Góngora was made of iron. He didn't react to my hint at all.

"Would it be foolish," he asked, "to attack a man with whom, just yesterday, we spoke so courteously?"

"Did we dine at your father-in-law's house?" I interjected with malicious ambiguity.

He didn't catch my drift. "Suppose that upon reaching a position of power, one feels the responsibility to investigate a man who only yesterday was, well, if not one's friend, then without doubt a respected acquaintance."

"Yes, I understand."

"And suppose that, upon reaching power, facts become known, evidence is presented that the friend, or acquaintance, as you say, is an evildoer. How do you like that?"

"I follow," I say, following a line to the wall. "I'm following you."

Góngora's metal-rimmed eyeglasses light up.

"What would you do, Señor Gorozpe?"

I put on my most affable expression. "Don't ask me; obviously this is your problem. I don't have enemies, you know? How 'bout you?"

"I have a government job. How do you like that?"

My look is a wordless question.

"And sometimes that forces me to take action, despite my nobler sentiments."

Now I really do offer a look of surprise with an element of mockery.

"Without even good manners," he confesses in a folksy manner. "How do you like that?"

"What do you intend to do?" I push the fingers from both hands together and raise them to my chin.

"No, not intend, Don Adam Gorozpe, I don't *intend to do, I do.*"

"So, what do you do?"

"I fulfill. How do you like that?"

"Who, or what do you fulfill?"

"My obligations."

"They seem to weigh on you."

"I even fulfill my obligations to my friends. How do you like that?"

"Your acquaintances."

"Yes. I can *ruin* them if I want to. How do you like that?"

"Well, go ahead, Señor Góngora. What's stopping you?"

He stood up. He said good-bye. He was already leaving my office when I stopped him and gave him a manly hug.

"I don't care whether they love me or hate me," he said, and left my office.

23

I can deduce many things from Adam Góngora's visit to my office. I'll limit myself to three observations and reactions: 1) Góngora wanted to intimidate me, to let me know that he is very powerful, as powerful as he is *short*, to invite an examination of his brutal track record, and to unsettle me with the question, When will it be your turn? That is, my turn.

I expected all this, and for the time being I'll limit myself to making two things clear: a) that I understand Góngora's intention, and b) that I am not going to step into his trap and let this diminutive person frighten me.

I need to figure out 2) what I can do to circumvent Góngora's evil intentions?

And the unspoken aspect is that 3) Góngora showed up as the hidden lover of my wife Priscila, the Queen of Carnival, without even hinting if he knew that I myself am not faithful to Priscila, and that Priscila, in all fairness, should have the right to the same erotic privileges as I do, especially considering that for twenty-one years, our relationship has come down to playing with scapulars that she uses to cover her genitals, without ever looking at mine.

Having said that, I have no lack of hypotheses concerning the Priscila-Góngora affair. As you know, my wife is a befuddled lady who speaks freely without the constraints of logic or reason. I'm sure that certain men would get turned on by an erotic encounter punctuated with Priscila announcing "Every man for himself!" or "Colgate, for sparkling-white teeth!" or "I'm walking along the tropical path!" or, more germane to the matter at hand, "Make ready the steel and the steed!" Ladies and gentlemen, I stand accused: has the force of habit made me oblivious to the secret sexuality of a woman who was desired by the most sought-after bachelors of her time? So *desired* in fact that, in the end, they did not marry her, sensing, perhaps, an edge in Priscila that I, miserable me, have been too dim to perceive or have mercilessly wasted?

I study my wife, but I can't put my finger on anything about her that would set her apart from the woman I've been married to for twenty-one years. Is it my fault? Could Priscila possess charms that I no longer appreciate, rendered senseless by force of habit? Do I need a new set of eyes—even eyes as myopic and unpleasant as Adam Góngora's—to see the virtues of Priscila, which I no longer recognize but that others still *do*?

Because of all this doubt, I am on the verge of making a desperate decision: to rediscover Priscila. Truth be told, *I have discovered* that I married her without love—allow me to confess to the simple scheme known around these parts as *mining for gold*—only so that I might have entrée into the world of high finance, as one only can if he's born rich or is married to a rich woman and living in the bosom of her prominent family.

This is my verdict: guilty as charged. I declare myself, *ab initio*, a scoundrel, a social climber, a despicable gold-digging man. And in so confessing I feel *cleansed*, washed clean of any sin carried out for the sake of my ascent in society, because of the feeling that maybe, if I thoroughly examined my soul, I would find the truth there, *another* truth: yes, I fell in love with Priscila, not with her money; yes, I desired her, and I felt victorious over the suitors who, as rumor has it, didn't want to marry her anyway.

Let's see, who says so? What if Priscila had been seriously courted by the Maserati boys, and had chosen the most luxurious driver? What if our history was such that—instead of me being her better-than-nothing guy who came across (by chance, by fate, by pity) his better-than-nothing gal—I had conquered her, stolen her away from the generic Maserati bachelors, and she had chosen me over the millionaires besieging her?

To quote Góngora's frequent punctuation: "How about that?"

Over the remains of old feelings that evaporated a long time ago, we construct reasons out of illusions. We are free to reconstruct the history of our love lives with the delusions permitted us by time. We embellish with ribbons what is in fact no more than a tree that has been dried up for twenty-one years. We—

I resist the movement of my soul, which awakens today and sets off toward Priscila the way it did, perhaps, twenty-one years ago. It's just that twenty-one years, *malgré* the philosophy of tango, indeed count for something, and I run the risk of inventing a sentimental life that I could never justify, because it had nothing to do with the start (and continuation) of my relationship with Priscila.

"You were never in love with her," I mentally reprimand myself. "You just wanted to climb the social ladder. You wanted security. You wanted the protection of a rich Priscila, that's all, you shameless son of a bitch . . ."

This self-flagellation ends when I tell myself that, whatever my initial motivation may have been to marry Priscila, the fact is that I have lived with her for more than two decades. We are *a couple*.

We are *married*. We are understood as such, and as such we are invited to parties, we are seated at the table, and we are forgiven—ugh!—Priscila's foul airs because—she needs no other license!—she is Adam Gorozpe's wife, which gives her the right to fart whenever and wherever she chooses . . .

But then, how to reconcile this sentiment with another that strikes me with a vengeance, unwanted, hidden in the secret depths of my life: my relationship with L? Can I reproach Priscila for her (alleged) love affair with Góngora while I devote myself to my (proven) love affair with L?

I am seized by fear. Following my line of reasoning, I overlooked the most important condition of my life. If you study my words (and I urge you to do so), you will note that, in the beginning, I said that Góngora seems to know that I am not faithful to Priscila and that my wife has the right, and so on . . . But no, Góngora has no way to know about my relationship with L. I have kept it absolutely secret; nothing in Góngora's attitude indicates that he knows about my life with L, *nothing*.

Or *everything*? Does he know everything, the innermost details? Can we keep no secrets from Góngora? Does he have us all caught in his dark fist of silver and amethyst rings?

Nothing, nothing gives me the certainty to assume that Góngora knows. And nothing indicates beyond any doubt that Góngora *doesn't* know.

Could this be the real treachery behind Góngora's visit to my office? To torture me by letting me imagine that he may or may not know about L? Because he can sleep with Priscila, and I can remain unmoved (that would be my aim, if it were so). He knows he can go after my financial interests, and I will remain unmoved because I am impervious to any local attack: my fortune is well safeguarded in places and instruments that I don't need to reveal here.

L is my weakest flank.

If Góngora attacks me there, he would be able to wound me . . . fatally, to the extent that he can't attack L without hurting me . . .

24

Another nightmare:

Adam González enters my dream.

He is a fat man with dark skin, curly hair, and a trumpet-player's lips.

This time, my nightmare happens very quickly, and the events unfold one after the other in flashes across the screen of my dream.

Adam González compiles a list of his enemies.

Slowly, he locks them up, one at a time.

He accuses one person of disrespecting our nation's flag, another of raiding the public trust, a third of abusing power, a fourth of insulting the omnipotent public figure Adam González.

In my dream—I am not fooled, this time I know *it's a dream*—those accused by González defend themselves.

"He attacks us just to humiliate us."

"He's sending a message to all citizens."

They understand the pronouncements.

"Nobody is safe from my arbitrary decisions."

"Nobody better think of turning against me."

"Nobody better protest, and nobody better ask for nothing."

The families of the detained state their cases.

"We haven't been allowed to see my father."

"My husband is in solitary confinement because he's guilty of being a flight risk."

"I know the jail cells. They measure two square meters. Nobody can lie down without bending their knees."

"I'm the governor. And they're going to take away the job that I was elected for."

"I'm a student. They locked me up for going to a demonstration."

"I'm the mayor. I've been waiting six years to be sentenced."

"We're guilty of treason, of rebellion, of sedition."

"We're disqualified."

"We're guilty."

"That's what Adam González says."

"If he says that, it must be so."

"God bless Adam González."

25

I return to L the way a parched man in the desert comes upon an oasis. Only now I am afraid. Have I been followed? Do they suspect anything? What does Góngora know? Are his bloodhounds on my trail?

Whereas before I saw only innocent glances, I now see suspicious glares. Actions that once would have seemed normal to me now seem the diversions of spies.

Why do all my associates wear dark sunglasses?

Why do I return to L, putting my lover in harm's way? Is Góngora following me? Does he know about my affair? Why am I going back? Just to say: "The situation has become very dangerous. We have to take a break for a while"?

And even as I compose the words, I'm not sure if they're true.

I've never told L a lie. L knows my life in detail: my feelings, my desires, and my fears. I love L because we can discuss what I would never dare let anyone else know. My relationship with Priscila and her family is—or has been up until now—strictly conventional. When my associates and I are finished discussing business, I become silent as a tomb.

L.

Only L knows all.

How am I going to say: "You have to understand, we need to take a break for a while," without having to answer the question,

"Why?"

"Why, Adam?"

"I can't tell you."

"You can't . . . ? I can't believe my ears."

"I can't see you for a while. I promise, it's for your own good."

"For my own good? Then why don't you give me a reason, Adam? What are you trying to pull?"

"I'm not trying to pull anything. I swear that I love you, and I swear that I don't want to put you in harm's way—"

"In harm's way? I know how to take care of myself."

"Look, this sounds like a Rorschach conversation. Just accept my reasons and—"

"But you're not giving me any reasons. You're only telling me 'we need to take a break for a while,' which means 'We're breaking up,' don't you understand? Why do you say such stupid things? Do you think I'm an idiot? Do you think that before I met you I never had any lovers? Do you think I never had a lover leave me? Do you think you're the first, you slime bucket, or the only one?"

L has never treated me this way, has never insulted me before. I have said it and repeated it from the beginning: our relationship is one of mutual respect, we tell each other everything.

Everything? When L rebukes me—"slime bucket"—I suddenly realize that I tell L everything, and L tells me *nothing*. What do I know about L? Where does L come from? Who are all these lovers L has been with?

"Why so secretive?" I ask myself and, to my surprise, say out loud.

L stares at me dumbfounded. I beg L not to repeat my phrase so we don't get back to the Rorschach test that this cursed encounter has become.

Curs-èd. Curs-ing. Un-helpful. What is the matter with me? Why did I need to announce to L that we had to "take a break for a while"? Have my circumstances rendered me an idiot? Why am I saying (L is right) these *stupid things*? Has Mr. Góngora with his borrowed haircut won the match before the game has even begun?

Am I so meek? Such a fool?

I was about to take it all back, to say, "No L, it's a joke, everything's just like it was before, nothing's happened, just like before, okay?"

But I can't. Nobody can take back an idiotic statement that was supposed to be honest.

I don't understand what has happened. I don't know why I have come to say to L: "We need to take a break for a while."

I forgot that for a lover the phrase *a break* elides the preposition *up*, that *a while* means *while we're alive*: I won't be seeing you anymore because we're breaking up. The lover cannot take this injunction as anything other than a deadly serious matter. I only wanted to shelter L from an attack on me, an exercise of Góngora's power that might have left L collateral damage. I understand this too late. I've already put my foot in my mouth.

L's words flow like a cascade of bile.

"For a *while*, you say? Liar. Tell the truth. *Forever*.

"Forever? No problem. I have no shortage of men.

"No shortage. Take the list of phone numbers. Call them, asshole. Go on, you can set up my dates.

"My dates? You're so naïve. Take a look at my calendar so that you can see how I manage my time when you're not with me.

"With me. Do you think that while you're in your office or celebrating a birthday with your stupid family, I sit around watching Luismi concerts?

"Luismi? Does Luismi make you jealous, you poor devil? Are

you jealous of a handsome singer who is admired by thousands of us human beings but with whom we thousands would never in a million years have any contact?

"Con-tact, tact. You can achieve anything with tact. What went wrong with you, Adam? How can you treat me like this? You and I, we're not like that."

The only sentence L said was, "You and I, we're not like that." The rest of the argument I invent, I imagine, because L's reaction is so unexpected to a suggestion that, seen in hindsight, was absolute assholishness on my part.

"You have to understand, we need to take a break for a while."

I told L because we tell each other everything. And now I realize that everything we say to each other is not only *pleasant*, but *shareable*. That's it: L and I share everything, and an important aspect of the "society" we've created, is that we tell each other everything, but everything that we tell each other brings us closer together.

Only today, only this time, faced for the first time with L's anger, I realize the truth.

I tell L *everything*: my business, my family, Abelardo left, Góngora showed up, and so on.

Everything.

And L tells me *nothing.*

What do I know about L?

Nothing.

Absolutely *nothing.*

L lives in the present and is *my present.*

L has never told me: I was born in *this place*, my parents were *such and such* . . . or I do *this and that* all day when you're not around, aside from watching TV and going to concerts at the National Auditorium.

I slam on my mental brakes.

And I? Have I told L that I was born in *this place*, my parents were *such and such*, where and how I grew up?

I haven't, have I?

In a certain sense, we're in the same position.

I know nothing about L's past. L knows nothing of mine.

Is that why we get along so well? Because we live only in the present, for the present? Because L knows everything I do today, and I know everything that L does at the same time?

Lovers of the present moment.

Lovers without a past.

Lovers who tell each other everything.

Only that until *today*, *everything* was the *usual*. There was nothing new. My business operates with certain special advantages, not of particularly fair- or free-market natures. In general, few fortunes grow, most people keep living in poverty, it's God's Law, and we'll always have our unanimous devotion to the Virgin of Guadalupe, who transcends ideologies and political parties, class distinctions, and bank accounts (or lack thereof).

My family is what it is, nothing new about that. The King of Bakery. The Queen of Spring. And what else? What do I know about L's past tense? What does L know about Adam's past perfect? Nothing, we choose the happiness of the present tense. We reject the traps of biography, psychoanalysis, gossip, and "what will people think." Our relationship goes back a long time, but it always begins *now*, in the moment . . .

But suddenly Abelardo runs away from The King of Bakery's house to become a "writer." And that damn Adam Góngora invades my life, poses riddles to me, conspires behind my back (his visit to my office confirmed this), and, to top it all off, plays footsie with my wife, Doña Priscila, the Queen of Carnival!

I reproach myself for my stupidity. This is not me. Everything that's happened has made me lose my bearings. I must recover control of the situation. The events at the office (Góngora's visit) and at home (Abelardo ran off, Priscila plays footsie with a police-executioner, an ill-mannered tyrant who speaks with his mouth full and lets food dribble down his chin) have diverted me from the road I follow, from the person I am. And from my privileged relationship with L, whom I've contaminated with my problems at home and at work, goddamn it!

I have to get myself together.

And why do my associates go around in dark sunglasses anyway?

"I am not about to let your *persona* consume mine," L says, cold as a Kelvinator. "I have my own life. Don't you try to change my personality. I always run from lovers who try to impose their will on me. Don't you even try it, you son of a bitch."

"There's no need to explain the changes in our personalities aloud," I argue, as I'm leaving.

Then L says something terrible. "If I kill you it's because I love you. And if I don't kill you, it's because I fear you."

And even though I am dressed, L gazes at my belly with fear, and, in an uncharacteristic way, with a lowered head, says: "Don't think that your personality is going to consume mine. I am not your *consommé* Adam. I can only be your rib."

26

Abelardo requests an appointment. At my office? No way, I answer, nobody from my family may enter the place where I work. That's the fundamental law of the well-organized life: separation of home and office.

At The Danube restaurant on Republic of Uruguay Street, we will eat shellfish, we will drink a nice bottle of Undurraga, and nobody will bother us now that the restaurant has been divided into small rooms to accommodate its Chinese clientele.

My brother-in-law tells me his troubles. He expresses them with a sensibility so poetic that I ask myself again, how did this orchid bloom in the midst of that cactus field? After having attended the Faculty of Arts and Ignacio Braniff's lectures, he fled the writer's tyrannical and closed circle and found asylum with Rodrigo Pola in the soap-opera universe. But that intellectual exile, he tells me, did not fill the great void in his heart. His heartache had begun at the Faculty, where the women surrounding the philosopher belonged to the Freudian Generation: they all wanted to match their lives with the experience of the psychiatrist's sofa, and their conversation aspired to the level of a psychoanalytic treatise; everything that wasn't psychoanalysis was banality, and the man who didn't take such monomaniacal anxiety seriously would not only be considered frivolous, but suspected of being—the horror—good in bed. They'd have nothing to do with virility. They feared being dominated. They wanted to tame the impotent man, treating him with enormous affection, searching for the secret reasons of his sexual malfunction: Father? Mother? Oedipus? King Laius? Don't lay us, Eddypus, Oedi Allan Poe? Blame it on the raven or being prematurely buried in the wrong coffin—or did the black cat *choose* to be sealed in the wall?

Worn out by the Freudettes, Abelardo sought in contrast the women he met through his work in television. He watched the shows, and despite the insipid dialogue (for which he bore some responsibility) some of the actresses seemed not only attractive, but even smart. However, he chose to associate with a homely one—that is, one who played the part of a homely woman—the little actress who was made up with braces on her teeth and peasant braids, and who usually said, "Yes, boss, whatever you say, boss," as the cameras rolled. Halfheartedly seduced, the actress in question turned out to be a bossy and foul-mouthed woman, and when Abelardo pointed out this contradiction to her, she treated him as a nincompoop for not understanding that an actress on screen is the opposite of what she is in real life and (as she pronounced the phrase) "vicey-versey." So if Abelardo wanted to find an angelic girl, he should seduce the *muwhahaha*-gloating villainess who sported the eye patch.

What a load of crap!

After these two failures, Abelardo, this young man in need of female companionship to compensate for the failure of his literary career, who had taken on the vocation of soap-opera script writer to make a living, felt another need as well: to become closer to God so that he might receive divine assistance and escape the contradictions that consumed him.

He began by attending evening mass at the Church of the Sacred Family in front of the Chiandoni ice cream parlor, which is where he'd taken his first communion (in the church, that is, not in the ice cream parlor).

One day, kneeling in the third row from the altar, he scrutinized the place. Only with great effort could he concentrate enough to pray. At that hour there was no service held in the empty church.

There was only a woman, kneeling in the first row.

From behind, he observed a long black veil covering her, from head to waist. The woman didn't move. Abelardo waited for her to make the slightest movement. She remained still. This worried Abelardo. He felt an impulse to go up to the first row and ask what was wrong. But his natural sense of discretion and the rules of courtesy—raised to the power of the Holy Trinity—stopped him.

He kept watch for five, ten, twelve minutes.

The woman didn't move at all.

Abelardo made up his mind. He rose from the third row and made his way to the first. He slid in next to the immobile woman. The great veil covered her face. He wondered what he should do? Touch her shoulder? Ask her, Ma'am, are you all right? Or be discreet and wait? To pray together in the otherwise empty church. Only, he didn't know—he needed to know—what the veiled woman was praying over. He couldn't hear anything, except for a faraway murmur. Her breath was no more detectable than her movement.

Then the voice of his father Don Celestino Holguín came to him in reproach, *coward, wimp, jerk-off,* while the invisible Priscila whimpered from behind the empty altar, *wine-fortified caramel, the three Magi, Insurgentes at the corner of . . .*

Abelardo realized, in the half-light of the Holy Family, that he'd unintentionally repeated his father's and his sister's phrases out loud, driven to a mysterious imitation that had let itself be heard, as if to substitute for the inaudible murmur of the pious woman kneeling beside him.

But when Abelardo said, *"Insurgentes at the corner of . . ."* the woman in question turned her veiled face toward him and finished his sentence: *"at the corner of . . . Quintana Roo."*

The rest is history.

27

Was it a comet? Or did the ground shake? Adam Gorozpe has a traumatic physical memory of the 1985 earthquake. He still hadn't married Priscila, and as a young student, he frequented a house on Durango Street called La Escondida, the Hideaway.

As at a cattle ranch, the new client was welcomed by the bell cow who paraded the young calves by lining them up for him in the living room.

"The customer chooses."

There was the usual variety. Skinny and fat. Young and not so young. With Chiclets and without Adams. Hardened and inexperienced. The young Adam chose the most nubile girl: with light-brown skin, hair long enough to drape her back all the way to her butt, a fake mole next to her mouth, greenish eyes, and a half-open mouth.

"What's your name?"

"Zoraida."

She didn't say, "Yes boss, whatever you say, boss," the way the maids in the soap operas did even then.

"Zoraida."

In the young Adam's mind appeared the image of the beautiful Moorish princess of the *Quixote*, described by Cervantes as a woman who arrives mounted on an ass, her face veiled and dressed in a brocade hat, with a long coat covering her from shoulders to feet, shouting "No, no Zoraida! María, María! Zoraida *macange!*" which means *not Zoraida, not at all.*

To say *no.* To be free.

To only say *yes.* Another type of freedom?

The symmetry that mirrored the literary Zoraida and this real live young woman unsettled the mind of Adam Gorozpe—an earlier incarnation of myself, the narrator, and of whom I speak in the third person because to be young is to be another person—to the point of doubting his purpose of sleeping with a woman who, at first sight, seemed ideal, but who was, as a result, untouchable. Or was that only a mirage? Zoraida didn't look like the other novices in the brothel. Was it only because she was *different* that she seemed *better*, and perhaps even a *virgin* like the character in the book and therefore *untouchable*? Yes or no?

Adam (who I am or who I was) looked for an answer in the girl's blue-green eyes and found only virgin wells of stupidity. Then he thought he saw all of those poor women whom Adam, single and lonesome, the lonesome and poor Adam, assuaged his male anxieties by frequenting, without even looking at them, convinced that, whether fat or skinny, ugly or beautiful, when the lights went off, it didn't matter: Adam sought and achieved a fleeting and instant satisfaction, different from masturbation only because his satisfaction was shared and therefore—despite all the warnings of the priests—less guilt-inducing than the heinous solitary pleasure that could lead to premature madness and eventually to sterility (as the priests taught that other man who was me).

"Don't pay them any mind," his teacher, the Colombian friar Filopáter, laughed. "Remember that your name is Adam. You are—you will always be—the first man. Your sin is not Eve. It's the apple. And the apple is greed, rebellion, and pride. Or your sin is knowledge."

Filopáter flashed a smile of either, I can't be certain, sarcasm or irony. The difference would be that sarcasm is stupid and easy, whereas irony is difficult and smart. I am grateful to Filopáter for the teachings I apply to my erotic life, the secret life shared with Zoraida and later with L. These teachings allowed me to feign ignorance, so that I could accept a lie masked as the truth until its eventual unmasking.

How could I apply the philosophical education given me by a teacher of religion to my sexual congress with Zoraida? By admitting that irony is the way to lessen the burden of what we can't deal with, and what we can't deal with is *truth*. Although the game doesn't end with this trope, nor for that matter begin with it, we use irony to entertain a lie in the guise of truth until it is exposed. Because too many lies are passed off as truth.

I am trying to explain the origin of my personality, which you have observed in action in my office, in my home, and unmasked with L. Now, though, the appearance in my life of the sinister thug Góngora, disguised as an agent of order, enhances my appreciation of irony as a movement of the spirit that I can use to resist that lizard-faced Góngora—with his nasty verbal mobility projected from a kind of inner cement—against whom I must use my own brand of irony, the irony of words that can seem like what Góngora is not, nor can be, irony with no defense against satire: to use language *a contrario sensu*, destabilizing truth in order to short-circuit life's absolutes.

Now more than ever I count on my *ironic* disposition as I confront Góngora's *malice*, his coarse winks, and his brazen vulgarity. Can I defeat him with the paradoxical weapon of irony, which subverts any pretense of absolute power—personified by Góngora—without running the risk of identifying myself with him because neither he—malicious—nor I—ironic—take anything too seriously? I trust that my irony will defeat Góngora's malice by employing, better than he can, three ways of being.

Greed. Rebellion. Pride.

Filopáter's words echoed in Adam's (my) mind with the resonance of a moral commandment. Greed, the desire to earn and to keep, didn't only refer to money, but also to personality, to worldly station. And this, one's station, was not inherited: it was earned thanks to the revolt against facts, against fate, against the place assigned by the lotteries of family, fortune, race, and geography. Pride consists in overcoming all those hardships to build a world of one's own, in which success cancels out the sin of greed and forgives the offense of rebellion.

All those ideas certainly crossed the mind of Adam Gorozpe (me, the one who is narrating, the one who is not me, but who I once was) at the speed of thought combined with the speed of the anticipated act of thrusting his (my) penis into the not-so-virginal-as-all-that Zoraida. This mixture of sex and thought was nowhere near as extraordinary as what happened next, without any intervention from Zoraida or (me) Adam.

The earth moved. What happened next was the great earthquake of September 19, 1985, during which a large part of Mexico City was destroyed, mostly the areas built over ancient lakes and canals, which that morning, while I lay with Zoraida, returned and reasserted their buried flow.

Lamps, ceilings, and furniture shook; hangers in closets rattled; images of the Virgin of Guadalupe in this room and all the other rooms of this Durango Street bordello crashed to the floor; china and vaginas rumbled; outside the whorehouse, bridges and roads vanished; and beyond, the city awoke astonished with itself, eyes opening to everything that the metropolis was and had been, as if the past were Mexico's sleeping ghost, the great Water God, who returns to life every so often, but, finding no outlet, no channel, becomes frantic and shakes his body, trapped between cement and adobe, until he slips through drains and rises from sewers, leaving a trail of destruction, which is just a cry of impotence from the memory of his ancient power, and, having completed his destructive work, he returns to his deep riverbed of dusty peace.

The fact is that, while fucking a beautiful young girl with blue-green eyes and loose hair, I, Adam Gorozpe, became trapped inside her vagina.

You heard me: *trapped*. Zoraida's vagina tightened out of fear and the basic feeling that something strange was going on, and I became a prisoner locked inside her box.

I don't know what happened. I felt the twin terror of an earthquake and a prison. I was not the master of my virility. Nor was Zoraida of her femininity. Realizing that my man's body and the body of a woman were stuck together like those of two stray dogs unable to escape their attachment, I was overcome with dread. Would I be attached forever to the beautiful Zoraida? Would I see her grow old, put on weight, become white-haired, and die before my eyes? Would death be the only possible escape from this carnal union? And Zoraida, would she also watch me grow old until I died in her arms?

Sure, these were macho fantasies. No erection lasts a lifetime.

Yet in that moment, this terror coexisted with a feeling of infinite pleasure, stretched out until the end, not just of the moment, but of time itself. My pleasure inside the woman would be, will be, eternal. Eternity would be pleasure, and who could hope for a better paradise . . . ?

Then three things happened.

The earth stopped quaking, and our bodies separated with a sigh, I know not whether of relief or regret. Either way, with agony.

I rose from the bed and drew the curtains to see air filled with dust, and to hear wailing sirens and a faraway cry.

Outside I saw that there had been an earthquake, and that now a heavenly body was passing across the sky. The morning had been violated by an earthquake and redeemed by a comet that followed the orbit of the rising sun. The comet's luminous tail spanned the city, the country, the whole wide world. But it pointed away from the sun in whose orbit it moved. It wanted to free itself from the sun.

I stepped away from the window.

Zoraida had gotten up.

She looked at my naked body, first with a sleepy sort of approval. Then she screamed.

28

Adam Góngora continues what the marvelous Rosario Castellanos would call his shadowy trade. He has emptied the prisons that he only just filled with lowlifes, beggars, cripples, and petty thieves.

"On the outside," he declares, "they're less dangerous."

But he leaves the innocent middle-class workers locked up.

"To set an example. The privileged are no longer so privileged, huh? How do you like that?"

Still the real criminals are free to do as they please, while Góngora numbs public opinion and his conscience (his what?), locking up and releasing all the innocent *lumpen* and the sex workers (I wonder what happened to the beautiful Zoraida) to create an image of efficient activity, which is deceptive, useless, and expeditious, for the public security forces. The awful problem is most people believe that, because Góngora does so many things, he must be doing something right. That's not the case. He's putting on one big farce.

How could I unmask Góngora?

Don't think, reader, that what I want to do to Góngora stems from a desire to take revenge on my damned namesake for seducing my wife. No, I am against Góngora because he has deceived the country. His repression doesn't affect the guilty. In fact, it protects them. As long as petty criminals are sent to prison, major criminals, now forgotten, are free to kidnap, to traffic in narcotics, and to murder.

How can I unmask Góngora? Above all, how can I punish him for his pervasive criminal farce without seeming to take revenge on him for having seduced my wife? This is a difficult problem that I am unable to solve until Góngora himself unintentionally offers me the answer.

Here's the problem: Góngora yields to the temptation of wielding power. For the record, he already has power. What I need to find out and prove is this: as powerful as a police czar might be, is there a power greater still?

Góngora is immersing himself in the deep and treacherous waters of politics. I suppose, given the enormous corruption of law enforcement, thanks to which half of the police officers are criminals, and half of the criminals are police officers, their various "jobs" interchangeable tasks, Góngora believes that by elevating this little game to the highest public level, he can seduce me and force me out of my very safe place as an influential corporate lawyer with no official position. I am already ideally situated. I don't know if Góngora is too crude to understand the advantages of my position, because one fine morning he shows up to offer me a *partnership*—his word—to install me (God have mercy!) as the president of the republic.

All the politicians, he tells me, are finished. They're useless. They have no idea how to govern. They don't know how to administer. He emphasizes each syllable: ad-min-is-ter, a verbal tic that I am more than familiar with from the speeches of my father-in-law, Don Celes.

"I have an idea," Góngora says from his unbelievable squatness.

"Oh!" I exclaim.

"What if you and I, my namesake, support an *impossible* candidate for the country's presidency? How do you like that?"

"How do you like that?" I reply. "You're saying you could improve the wheel by making it round."

"No, I'm serious, what if you, who are the economic force, and I, who am law enforcement, come together to back an impossible candidate? How do you like that?"

I doubt that I'll like the plan. "What do you mean *impossible*?" I ask. "Impossible because the candidate is a blockhead, dishonest, or . . . ?"—I have to think before I can conclude my question—"Or because he is unthinkable?"

Góngora tries to smile. He can't say what he's thinking. He runs his hand over his head, adjusting his borrowed hair.

"No, *impossible* only so the *possible* one can thank him. How do you like that?"

I admit that Góngora's mental carousel makes me dizzy. When I recover my senses, I also recover logic.

"And who, then, would be the *possible* one?"

"Whoever is the power behind the throne. How do you like that?"

"You know, Góngora, we already had a *Maximato*, and back then the president lived in the Palace and the guy in charge lived across the street."

"Sure. Calles was the Supreme Boss, and the presidents were his puppets."

"So, history repeats itself? Is that what you believe?"

"Nuh-uh, counselor. Not at all. Because this time whoever occupies the chair owes it not just to one Supreme Boss, but to two. How do you like that?"

Pregnant pause!

"To you and me. You are the impossible one so that we can both be possible . . . How do you like that?"

"And who will be the president?"

"You, of course, my dear counselor. It couldn't be otherwise. How do you like that? I'm not trying to trick you."

Góngora leaves, imagining that he has, if not convinced me, at least intrigued me enough that I will consider his proposition. He's dead wrong. In less than two minutes I figure out that this idiot thinks he's smart, that he has become drunk on the sweet nectar of power, that he has no idea with whom he's dealing—Adam Gorozpe—and that perhaps, this stone-age Don Juan believes that forming an alliance with me transforms his love affair with Priscila into, I don't know, a *ménage-à-trois*, which would not stop it anyway from being a ridiculous burlesque.

P.S. I invite Abelardo Holguín to lunch at the Bellinghausen. He arrives, as usual. But there is something different about him, something about him that I don't recognize.

29

I don't know. Not knowing disturbs me. It's even more disturbing not to know what I thought I knew. Why are my business associates wearing dark sunglasses? I've been clear on this issue: I am not going to lower myself to their level; I'm not going to ask them. If they want to put on little blind-man faces, that's a reflection on them.

My family relations wear, if not sunglasses, then blinders, like the ones coachmen fit on their horses' heads to block their peripheral vision, so they can trot straight ahead without being frightened, as though all were well with their world.

My relationship with L is looking ugly, pretty ugly.

Priscila is on cloud nine. She floats. She still talks nonsense, and now she looks more stunned than ever, as if her new situation had left her bedazzled. Before, her indifference to cause and effect was spontaneous—a part of her—but now it seems, paradoxically, tied to some reality that I try to understand as she walks up the stairs, arms raised, her robe trailing, while she proclaims, "I am the Queen of Spring," then pauses on the landing to slap the new maid who is descending with a stack of clean towels.

On another day, I catch Góngora in the small living room, kneeling before Priscila, as if a dwarf like him would need to get down on bended knee to declare his love. Even standing, that measly little man seems to be kneeling.

He could have been saying anything, because she kept whispering, "Go on, tell me more . . . Tell me more . . ."

This idiotic request makes me think that Góngora and Priscila are still experiencing the first blush of love. Perhaps he's still courting her, and while she lets herself be loved by him, they've yet to jump each other's bones or into bed. But there is ample room for doubt: What about Priscila's lies when she disappears for the afternoon? Does she sleep with Góngora, or do they drink milkshakes at Sanborns, a saintly couple like Mickey Rooney and Judy Garland in some of the movies I like to discuss with Abelardo?

Whatever their relation, Góngora straightens up when he hears my footsteps and, because he is no fool, he greets me politely. But Priscila, who is one, exclaims, "Oh, Mr. Góngora was only tying his shoe. Brazil, Brazilian, land of samba and . . ."

I stare at Góngora's shoes with a disdain that turns to admiration when I remember that he doesn't wear cuban heels.

I greet him with a nod of the head and leave, thinking that, after all, I would be hard-pressed to give a flying fuck what Priscila and Góngora are up to. That's their problem; I can't think of a better punishment for both than to become each other's lovers. I realize, with a disappointed sigh, that I have no interest in them.

What really has me upset is the situation with L.

We've never been as distant as we are now. My problems at my office (the mystery of the dark sunglasses) and at home (the transparent relationship of Góngora and Priscila) are minor.

L, however, has been *my life*. This is easily said but—at the risk of sounding redundant—nobody can prove or give meaning to the expression unless he *lives that life*. My relationship with L, interrupted by my ill-conceived remark the other day ("You have to understand, we need to take a break for a while."), brings me back to earth, in the sense that, until now, I have always been the *winner*. Do my readers understand me? Everything has gone well for me, without my even wishing for it; whatever I do, things turn out in my favor.

You can call me King Midas or Rothschild or Trimalchio and even defame my profession ("The first thing we do," said a real dick, "let's kill all the lawyers"), but the truth is that I put effort into what I do, and I realize that my actions only succeed because of some unforeseen element in them, an element of chance, a fortune that favors me without my having to imagine it.

My good fortune is understood publicly, and that's fine. What nobody but me knows is the source of my good luck. My good luck, the source of my good luck, has a name and a voice: L. Without L, everything else would fall apart. Or if everything existed, it wouldn't be worth a pile of beans. I'm not saying anything that the reader doesn't know. Each of us understands that there is a private value that affects the external value of things. Having money, professional success, friends, and all the good things in life is ultimately based on the existence of a fundamental loving relationship. Be it with one's father or mother; with both; with one's children; with one's closest friends; with some teacher (Filopáter). Nothing grows without that seed. To love and to know that one is loved. To understand that, even if we lack everything and the world is falling apart, if we end up in the street, *whatever happens*, we have the *ground* from which to start over again. No man—and John Donne probably meant *no person*—is an island. We have to share our island with someone we love, or else we live alone. The Robinson Crusoes of this world don't grow on trees; most of us rely on the basic affection of one person or two or five people. But as long as just one person loves us, we won't perish completely.

I describe my relationship with L. I do so in a tone unheard of for me, almost confessional, the tone introduced by Job himself, who confesses before God and in doing so writes his autobiography, which turns life into fiction to better *impress* God as well as, incidentally, the mundane audience to which he claims he doesn't aspire and to whom, however, he implicitly appeals: *Listen to me, I am Job, the soul of pain and patience.*

How to make a confession to the world? Shouting? Articulating? Imagining it? Letting *others* do the job?

I read Lucretius with Filopáter and learned that if God exists, he is not in the least interested in human beings. (Filopáter paid a high price for saying this, and for adding Plato's heresy: that if God exists, we lose hope because the gods only favor humanity when it loses its mind).

A crazy god and a sinner, what a pair! "The soul is too small to contain itself," says Saint Augustine. That is why it must create a chamber in the amplified expressive form called *the confession*, an unthinkable genre for the Greeks who preceded him and who sought the harmony of truth, not its willful distortion by a harried heart like mine. For that, Saint Augustine chooses memory, a bitter and uncertain memory, to recover—he says—what he has forgotten.

That is why I'm not a saint. I have chosen *to have no memory*, and it is high time that the reader learned this. I don't want what I remember. I don't remember what I want. Why? Perhaps because the purpose of all biographies, as Filopáter one day told me, is to appear to be something real rather than fictitious. The biography would be the work of reason, not feeling, a storm the biographer must leave behind.

Saint Augustine's city is the City of God. It was Father Filopáter's city. I live in the City of Man, where a policeman known as Adam Góngora kneels before my wife, Priscila Holguín, both of them trying to throw me off the trail on which I would only find out what I already know. The heart has its reasons, and reason ignores those reasons. The heart wants to break free of its prison, and Góngora lives in the prison of the most banal rationality, a real equivalent of the prisons of San Juan de Aragón and of Santa Catita, which contain the prisoners of a disciplinary neogongorism that doesn't know that the heart has its own history and so can't know that this personal history cannot be exhausted by biography, philosophy, or politics, because its purpose, as incredible and impossible as it seems, is nothing more and nothing less than to regain paradise.

Paradise Regained.

L's love regained.

How do you like that?

30

In the ongoing dispute about comets, Father Güemes (who finally revealed his name) claims that each passing of the asteroid has been a fateful sign: 1965, the beginning of the end of the PRI (Party of Revolutionary Institutions) and presidential arrogance; 1957, the end of the "Mexican miracle" and the loss of the last revolutionary illusions; 1910, during the revolution, need I say more, Madero enters Mexico City, there is an earthquake, and the comet passes; 1908, in the tower of Chapultepec Castle, the old dictator Porfirio Díaz, watching the passing of the comet, announces that Mexico is ripe for democracy and leaves his extravagant moustache to soak; 1852, the passing of the comet coincides with the end of Santa Anna's dictatorship and the start of the liberal revolution; 1758, the comet is the portentous light of the still-to-come revolution for independence from Spain; 1682, the viceroy of La Laguna, Count of Paredes, will soon order the hanging of Antonio Benavides, a seafaring pirate whose life ended on the dry plateau, in the small square of El Volador, all because he deliriously gave himself the nickname "the Hidden," proof positive, because surprise candidates in presidential elections were called "hidden candidates," that every past contains its future; 1607, this time the comet, alleges Güemes, prefigures and celebrates good government, when Luis de Velasco, the younger, in his second term as viceroy of New Spain, enforces the abolition of Indian slavery, but fights along Río Blanco Road against Yanga and the other runaway black slaves, whom he would later pardon and to whom he would give a new city in Veracruz to be called San Lorenzo de los Negros; in contrast, in 1553, the comet coincides with the catastrophic flooding of Mexico City, proving that its crossing of the sky equally celebrates joys and announces tragedies; and in 1531 (the man of faith now reaching the end of his reoccurring sermon), the comet and the Virgin appear at the same time, heralding the end of paganism; "Faith has prevailed, my esteemed Don Vizarrón," and the scientist Vizarrón who didn't want to be outdone by the prelate and so revealed his name, too, answered, "Yes, but in 1508, when there was no Christianity in Mexico nor prudes of your sort, my dear Don Güemes, the meteor arrived with thunderbolts, the Aztec temples burned, the commotion troubled its waters, the wind mingled its lamentations with those of The Weeping Woman, La Llorona, who roamed the streets of the city every night screaming, *Oh my children, oh my children . . .* "

"That just goes to prove what I was saying," explains the preacher.

"The comet was a sign that Christ was already on his way."

"That's cheating," Vizarrón laughs, "pure sophistry. What do all the comets have in common? I'll tell you: it's not history, it's physics. The comet travels in an elliptic orbit of the sun. It is made, my dear sir, of ice and rock. It generates a gaseous exterior. It tail stretches millions of miles. It ejects stellar particulates. The comet is a product of the sun. But it doesn't reflect sunlight. It reflects solar radiation, which is different; it emits its own light. Fleeting light, my good man. When the comet nears the sun, it vaporizes. It ceases to exist."

"But it coincides with historical events. It is an outward manifestation of the coincidence of faith with facts."

"You're the one who mixes history and miracle, miracle and comet. You might like to know that nine comets pass each year. What have you got to say to that? What are you going to tell me now?"

Nothing could answer that but the voice of Adam Gorozpe's gardener (that's mine, the narrator's gardener) concentrating on his work:

Oh, comet, if you'd only known
What you'd come to herald
You never would have shown
Lighting up the heavens.
Nobody would blame you.
Not God, who sent him to you.

31

While trying to devise a plan to defeat Góngora, a simple visit gives me the answer.

The diminutive janissary is coming to see me on some evil errand. I consult with one of my business advisors whom I have asked to attend our meeting, which ought to let Góngora know that there are no secrets between us. If he wants to propose something to me, he can say it in front of a witness. I've had enough of his petty palace intrigues: that we'll both govern, who's going to be number one and who's going to be number two, that either number one is going to be the figurehead for number two or we are going to treat each other as equals, only I, a civilian, am much more convincing as Chief of State than a soldier, militarism being over, the president has to be a civilian, and so on and so on and on. Let's see if Góngora dares to propose any of his crooked plots in the presence of a third party.

On entering the meeting room, the Lilliputian conceals his displeasure at the presence of another person.

"Don Diego Osorio," I introduce my associate, as he removes his sunglasses. "Don Adam Góngora."

Góngora makes a good-afternoon gesture to wave good-bye to my associate, who, following my instructions, takes his seat again, to Góngora's now noticeable chagrin. In the conspicuous silence, an angel passes over the table. My associate offers Góngora a cigarette. Góngora declines. My associate puts the cigarette in his mouth and, extending his arm as though to see if it works, he lights his cigarette lighter near Góngora's face.

The flame barely touches Góngora's cheek, but he looses a hair-raising scream of agony, terror, exorcism, fear, fear, fear.

The little man sits up and raises his arms involuntarily as protection from the lighter's harmless little flame.

His face is the classical image of terror.

I look at him. We look at each other.

Góngora's eyes reveal his fury at having been caught in a moment of weakness. My associate closes the lighter. He understands my look. He understands my gestures. Again he lights the lighter. Plays with it. At my silent signal, he moves the flame near Góngora's face. Góngora stares at me with deep hatred. He raises a hand in defense. He dares not extinguish the source of his terror. He hides his hand. He covers his eyes with the other hand. Any composure that he'd reserved is now lost. He turns his back on us. He flees my office.

"Thank you, Diego."

My business associate puts on his dark shades again, which he'd had the courtesy to take off to give Góngora the impression that everything here was under control.

But why are all my employees still wearing dark sunglasses?

32

The scene I just described, ladies and gentlemen, strengthened my confidence that had been shaken during the roller coaster of emotions that I have described so far. So many recent situations seemed designed to set me off. The black sunglasses worn by my associates. My poor Priscila's romantic rebirth. The military menace of Adam Góngora.

But my most immediate concern was how to work out my screwed-up relationship with L. I could easily dispense with my business associates, my wife, or any frigid lovers; I just couldn't go on without L.

I'm of two minds about what to do for L and me. Should I make peace with myself before going back to L and announcing what I can only say if I've already said it to myself?

Or should I rely on the spontaneity of our encounter and without preconceptions show myself in front of L standing naked, so to speak, not unlike the first man on the first day: Adam and L?

Dear reader who accompanies me through these trying times, I don't know how to choose between these two strategies. They become confused in my mind. No wonder, because they are mutually exclusive approaches to—two versions of—the same moment, and to borrow a bullfighting term, the moment of truth has come.

L: you have accepted me as a proud man. You accept me because you know that, in contrast to everyone else, my pride is not based on arrogance or narcissism. Besides, I don't know if one or the other of those despicable traits even deserves the name of pride. Arrogance is nothing more than an empty pose for the benefit of others. Arrogance doesn't come from the arrogant person's soul, and it has only one purpose: to impress and humiliate third parties, which makes the arrogant man stand out more while hiding just how vacuous he is.

As for Narcissus, we know him as a man in love with his own reflection. Is this the idea that we identify with the most, darling? A young and beautiful man is condemned to be unable to see himself, but only to be seen by others. The gods have given him the love of everything and for everything, but they've denied him self-love. Narcissus is condemned to have and yet not to have. That is why his lover is Echo, a mere repetition of the other's scream.

Echo is alone, L, her voice is the echo of an echo. And her lover was made the ancient promise that he would live to a ripe old age, as long as he never saw himself. He doesn't know that this is a divine privilege, to grow ever older, but not to be allowed to see the reflection of passing time. To *know* that he has grown old, perhaps, but never to *see* himself old.

The price Narcissus pays is that he can't love anybody. To be loved but not to love. To be loved by an echo, a repetition. Why, if they say that I am so beautiful, can I never see myself or love somebody? Why am I only loved by an echo? Who am I?

You know, L, Narcissus is neither arrogant nor proud. He is at once curious and ashamed of his curiosity. He sees himself reflected in a pool of spring water. He falls in love with his own image. He becomes a captive of himself, of his appearance, of his reflection.

L, just imagine Narcissus's anguish when he discovers beauty but can't possess it, because beauty is only a reflection in the water and that reflection is him, Narcissus himself, an elusive and ungraspable liquid . . .

Pride is a manifestation of dignity. The most selfish—but not the least important—thing about dignity is that a dignified person can be proud even if he is modest, and I have always asked myself if modesty isn't another disguise taken up by pride. Modesty, especially when it replaces humility, can conceal a diabolical pride merely biding its time to show itself naked and sporting a devil's tail.

I tell myself all this so I can present myself to L, cognizant not just of my own worth, but also of L's.

How much ground must L and I cede to each other to re-establish our relationship? But then again, maybe a relationship is not about, is not saved by, ceding, at least not under duress, but rather *conceding*, without saying a word, with an absence of any sense of victory, or defeat, through a *gesture* of rapprochement, a *movement* of affection, an *attitude* that says "nothing happened here"—while knowing that something did happen—and goes on to say "let's go back to being who we were before."

Is this so? Would an absolution of previous mistakes allow us to begin our relationship anew, or should L and I be resigned to endure, now and forever, memories of the times we were absent from each other's lives.

I might be avoiding the easiest and most direct formulation: L and I love each other. L and I need each other. In the heat of our argument, L said no, admitted having a past, admitted having a life without me, and admitted being able to live without me. I never said anything of the sort. That doesn't give me license to appear, now, as the offended party. I have to admit that getting these things out in the open was good for L, and part of the evil of losing love.

I don't know if I'm just kidding myself by pretending that all this necessarily implies arrogance or narcissism. Perhaps the way to overcome this danger is to be persistent, if persistence is an implied tribute to the beloved and not a rude insistence we foist upon a person whom we desire but who doesn't desire us. I'm sure I've come upon the best way to allow L and me to start over.

How will I know if it will work? I mustn't kid myself. I'll only know when I appear before L in the difficult position of admitting what happened, but not apologizing, banking on the fact that L, as much as I, wants us to get back together, because we know everything about each other.

There are relationships between two people who don't know much about each other. These can be flash-in-the-pan or long-lasting relationships, because getting to know your partner takes a lifetime. Until recently, my relationship with L had grown more significant because I felt that the more things I knew, the more I could affirm and confirm. Did this certainty lead me to toy with L's feelings?

"We need to take a break for a while," I had said, without realizing that my words were superfluous: everything that led me in that moment to utter them to protect L and to save our relationship— from political and family forces, from the threats accumulating like clouds, Góngora, Priscila, Abelardo, the criminals, the injustices, the insecurity, Jenaro Rubalcava, Chachacha, Big Snake, my father-in-law, the Boy-God of Insurgentes, my associates wearing

sunglasses in the office—in the end turned out to be banal, fictitious, feathers in the wind.

And they nearly destroyed our love.

Will I be able to reinvent it?

P.S. #2: I called Abelardo's office at the network.

They answered: "He doesn't work here anymore."

"Why not?"

"I can't say."

"Where did he go?"

"Who knows?"

33

Now I know Adam Góngora's secret: he's afraid of fire. He doesn't know my secret. He'll never see me naked. I must begin my siege of him while doubts still besiege me. Why should I get rid of Góngora when he is doing me the favor of distracting Priscila, rejuvenating her, and flirting with her—abilities I lost a while back? If the sole function of the other Adam were to do what this Adam doesn't want to and can't do (seduce Priscila), I would leave him alone.

Unfortunately Góngora is not only Priscila's lover-boy, but also the guardian of order, and the order that he protects is a monstrous lie. He accuses the innocent and protects the guilty. He locks up petty offenders and rich people and businessmen. But he doesn't touch—not even with the proverbial ten-foot pole—the gang and cartel leaders, the gunrunners, and the criminals who extort and kidnap.

It's painful to accept his tactics, but public opinion, hungry for action, applauds action of any kind, action for action's sake. All of Góngora's proclamations bring forth massive rallies of white-clad people demanding the punishment of criminals. Góngora appeases and pleases them by jailing the indigent and, on occasion, one or two millionaires. To set an example. And what about the newly disenfranchised middle class? They're off to the *Gorozpevilles*.

Under this public security administration, real criminals are left in peace, and that gives me a chance to act against Góngora, which his stupid courtship of my wife Priscila wouldn't justify.

I'll try a ruse to get him to drop his defenses.

I play dumb. I summon Góngora to my office, and I tell him that I agree with his plan: to see if we can take power with Adam (me) in the presidential seat and Adam (him) as the power behind the throne.

Góngora smiles with a crooked mouth worthy of Dick Cheney.

"The truth, oh my namesake," I tell him as I get close enough to smell his hellish breath. "The truth is that my wife, Priscila, has fallen in love with you."

I would have liked to photograph Góngora's face: feigned surprise, intense satisfaction, and the tics of a sinister lady-killer. And candid caution.

"You don't say. Really?"

"I'm telling you—and look, I won't be the one to come between you . . ."

"What are you saying?"

"No, not me. I don't have a problem with the two of you as a couple. The only one who'd be a problem for you would be my father-in-law, Don Celestino Holguín."

"A problem?"

"Yeah, a problem."

Góngora's laugh is awfully grave. "I don't know the meaning of the word *problem*. How do you like that?"

"Don Celes is a daily-communion-taking, breast-beating Catholic."

"Well, that's good."

"No, that's bad. He's never going to allow his daughter to divorce."

"How do you know?"

"Because I tried."

"I know that you don't satisfy Priscila. How do you like that?"

"Nor does Priscila satisfy me. There you have it. The problem is that my father-in-law won't allow a divorce. He likes to say that 'marriage is forever' and or at least 'until death do us part.'"

Pregnant pause.

"Góngora, have you seen the bedroom of Priscila's mother, the late Doña Rosenda?"

"Priscila was kind enough to—"

"So you see the cult of marriage that Don Celes professes? Even after death. You understand, don't you? He'll never allow his only daughter to get a divorce."

"Of course he will. Sometimes he passes through the living room while I'm taking tea with Pris—"

"Get behind me, Satan, because there's nothing here for you."

"That's it," Góngora said, trying to hold me in his moist gaze. "That's exactly what he says. What the hell does that mean anyway?"

"My good Mr. Góngora, that means our common enemy goes by the name of Don Celestino Holguín."

"Your father-in-law," Góngora says with an appropriateness that must have rubbed off on him from Priscila. "How do you like that?"

"But not yours," I say interrupting Góngora's daydream.

"Let's see, let's see how to handle this," my namesake says, leaning in while I, as though not interested, light a match in his face.

P.S. #3: Abelardo leaves me a message. "Lunch tomorrow at half-past two at the Bellinghausen."

34

In the midst of this growing tension between truth and lies, between comedy and drama, I wonder if *what I'm doing* is changing into *what I ought to do* in order to save the families, to save their food, their houses, and their belongings, on which I've made, I realize, *my fortune*.

Because what I am doing is not a personal favor or some random act. I know what's going on. The physical presence of Adam Góngora is proof of what's going on and puts me under the gun, because I have to stop him.

But how?

Perhaps by doing the opposite of what he does.

Though I am disgusted by the prospect, I need to employ some of the tactics Góngora uses and take them to an extreme. To defeat Góngora I must deceive him, first with arguments as childish as those I just offered him about Don Celes's opposition to divorce. Then I will need to carry out actions that Góngora could not equal, let alone surpass, in their brutality.

Ours is a country of recently made fortunes. In colonial times the clergy and landowners, perhaps, took extra large slices of the domestic pie, but they always left the people's table with more than just crumbs. But after Independence, that table lost its legs. Without the protection of the Spanish Crown, the new republic became a *Donnybrook* nation, a pilgrimage to hell in a handbasket in honor of the Amozoc Virgin of Rosario, a *chienlit*, a bordello, a disaster area, or an orchestra whose sole music was the clicking prosthetic footsteps of the dictator Santa Anna. Juárez and the liberals defeated the conservative order, Maximilian's empire, and the French occupation. Ever since, Mexico has struggled to reconcile order and movement, institutions and ascent. The millionaires of my childhood were paupers compared to the today's millionaires, but the new ones live in a very diverse, very large society of more than a hundred million people fighting to move up in the world and, by hook or by crook, to take their place in the sun.

I'm a lawyer and an investor. I am familiar with the work of doctors, jurists, architects, teachers, scientists, journalists, businessmen, and even a politician or two who are a credit to our country. But I also know about the eternal rites of national corruption from the top to the bottom, from the lion to the coyote, from the eagle to the serpent it eats on the national seal. Big or bite-size bribes are the currency in the accumulation of influence, winks and offers "that you can't refuse." From the bribe for the police officer to the bribe from the minister. The first, so that he won't send you to the slammer. The second, so that you won't send him to the slammer. Man, this country is screwed up!

No, what's perverse and awful here is just the new criminal class that is slowly usurping power, beginning at the northern border then moving to the interior, first corrupting the illiterate police officer, then the educated politician, all without personal intermediaries. Where do these new criminals come from? They aren't from the peasant- or working- or middle-class. They belong to a separate class: the criminal class, born, like Venus, from the foam of the sea, or in their case, from the foam of a warm beer spilled in a seedy cantina. They are the children of the comet. They corrupt, seduce, blackmail, threaten, and end up taking over a town, a state, and one day the entire country . . .

Alas, sometimes, to safeguard what is good one must resort to the worst.

And that's what I must do now.

I find myself, ladies and gentlemen, between a need and a requirement. Allow me to distinguish between those two. A *need* can be postponed. A *requirement* cannot. The way I see it, there is a need for a better, more just society. To achieve this, I am required to execute a brutal plan that will draw attention to and obviate Adam Góngora's own brutal actions.

The stinky little man inadvertently provides me with an excuse. In the back of my mind, there was already this warning: Góngora is very clever, more than clever. And he might just be *too* clever.

He was.

The master plan of the other Adam (that is, Góngora) consists of occupying empty political spaces, spaces ceded by local governments. He takes over those spaces fast, with the power of law enforcement. When local governments become paralyzed because of crime, arms- and drug-trafficking, or the plain and simple absence of authority, Góngora sends armed occupiers to patrol public buildings, sets machine gun nests on the rooftops, and—I fear—intends to dissolve Congress, to line up and execute the innocent and the petty criminals, and then to set the dangerous ones free to join him and his men to form—I might as well call it what it is—a fascist army.

Is Góngora's plan the solution to our worst problems? Is it folly or reason? Am I guessing or am I foreseeing?

How much do I really know, and how much do I merely imagine?

Let's say that the seen and the foreseen share in the truth. But Góngora, hungry for power—*measured* power—beats around the bush of a floral temple more baroque than Tonantzintla and perpetrates a crime that, in one fell swoop, kills two birds with one stone.

This is where his intelligence, clouded by love, fails.

He thinks he's uncovered my weakness. He believes that I hate my father-in-law Don Celes, the King of Bakery. My father-in-law alone is in the way of Góngora and Priscila's union and Priscila and my separation. Don Celes doesn't want to know about divorce. *Get behind me*, as he likes to say.

For his and my benefit, Góngora is preparing to do away with Don Celes.

But Góngora doesn't know that there is no such thing as a perfect crime. I know. That is the difference between an educated man (myself, if I may say so) and an ignorant brute like Góngora (a donkey that plays the flute while conducting an orchestra).

Here is Góngora's criminal plan, and where it goes wrong.

Góngora orders his henchman Big Snake, provisionally released from jail thanks to Góngora's intervention, to murder Don Celes while, carefree and indulging his sweet-tooth, he makes his weekly rounds of his pastry shops. But Big Snake, instead of killing Don Celes, murders the wrong baker, one who makes the same rounds as the boss, and, realizing his mistake, Big Snake lies to Góngora, saying that he fulfilled his part of the bargain and killed Don Celes, and that now Góngora should make good on his word and free him once and for all from the dark prison of San Juan de Aragón.

Don Góngora arrives at the Lomas Virreyes house dressed in black to offer his condolences to his alleged girlfriend, my wife

Priscila. He is unnerved at the absence of black bunting at the entrance of the Catholic home, and he practically goes apoplectic when the door is answered by Don Celestino Holguín himself, alive and kicking and with a scowl on his face.

"Come in, Janissary," he says not very politely to a perplexed Adam Góngora. "Move it, before the tea gets cold, and don't trip over the rugs. They're genuine Persians."

35

I meet Abelardo Holguín for lunch at the Bellinghausen. He's reserved a table for four, which only he and I will sit at, in the restaurant's upper level, from where we can see and be seen but not hear or be heard. (The owner refuses to divide the restaurant into cubicles appropriate for the clients he refers to as *los fumanchú*.)

There's something different about Abelardo. Something flamboyant about him. He's always been an elegant young man. Now, his elegance dazzles and puzzles me. It's not like him. The discretion he had exhibited at Don Celes's house seems diminished and replaced by a strange sort of glow. I suppose that working in television has given him the idea that he must have his own look, so I try to ignore it. But when I called his company, they assured me that he no longer worked there.

"Did you change jobs?" I ask him.

"No," he smiles, "the job changed me."

I respond with my please-explain look.

He offers a lengthy explanation that manages to showcase the breadth of his talent for literary discourse. I have met young writers who wander about lost, taking baby steps without much success, until one day they realize that though they won't take off in literature, their facility for literary rhetoric gives them wings to fly away to other less demanding but better endowed nests.

Abelardo's explanation has to do with the state of the republic, a subject that I know something about, as do you, especially if you've read this story so far. The nation is adrift. We have lost our faith in everything. The government can't tell an A from a windmill. The political parties are too busy fighting each other to propose any solutions to our problems. The halls of parliament have become places to take a nice siesta, to assault speakers, and to display banners. Several state governments are controlled by drug traffickers, and others are subject to Adam Góngora's armed forces. Tourists have been scared away. The price of oil is falling. At the border migrants can no longer migrate, and there are no indispensable jobs for them in Mexico despite the need everywhere for construction and reconstruction: highways, ports, dams, development of the tropics, agricultural development, urban renewal . . .

I nod. He asks the perpetual question: what can we do to fix our country?

I start to answer, case by case, industry, commerce, and so on.

He interrupts me with innocence and disdain.

"Projects and more projects, Adam. We know them all. Every project is left unfinished. Good intentions are frustrated by apathy, greed, carelessness. If I already have what's mine, why should I care about others . . . ? That's how my father thinks, and don't tell me he doesn't."

He gives me a harsh look.

"And what about you, Adam?"

I answer him that I am a lawyer and a businessman who generates wealth and offers jobs, savings, and pensions, and I—

"But what about our soul, Adam? The spirit of this country?"

I don't know how to answer him. I already spoke my mind. I believe in investment, work, progress, what . . . ?

"And the soul?" Abelardo again insists. "What will become of our soul?"

Because the answer to this question must be serious, I will need to think it through. The soul . . . Well . . . There's still time for that . . . All eternity, after all?

Unlike the fate of the nation's soul, my situation at home needs urgent attention.

I have to deal with Priscila: Abelardo's sister, Don Celestino's daughter, Góngora's (likely) lover, and my wife before man and God.

Enmeshed as I have been in the puzzling dramas described here, it's been ages since I've been alone with my wife. She's been constantly courted by Góngora, and except as relates to him, she hasn't been on my mind much. I suppose things will continue this way until they reach some sort of a natural conclusion.

But Priscila confronts me later in the afternoon.

"Does it surprise you that I love an ugly man?"

"No," I respond calmly, "in spite of appearances, the ugly ones seem to have more luck than the good-looking ones."

"Rumba is more pleasant than son," she continues, seemingly at random.

"What's that? Be more coherent, for the love of—"

"That I love an ugly, dirty man. That I've had it up to here with your cleanliness. Everything about you is clean and washed. In Jalisco they want good, clean elections . . ."

"That's your business," I say, trying to bring down the curtain on this theater of the absurd.

"'I am the winner!' 'Along the tropical trail!'"

"You're a poor imbecile," I blurt out.

"I am the Queen of Spring restored to my throne! Cantinflas!"

"Well, as the song goes, *dead leaves gather in oblivion . . .*'" "*You can no longer defeat me,*" Priscila says, expanding like a male peacock. "Because you can't defeat your rival, *over at the big ranch, where I used to live . . .*"

"You realize, don't you, that Góngora is just using you?"

"He loves me. He says he wishes I was his birthday piñata."

"So he could break you open with a stick?"

"No, to fill me up with candy."

"To fill you up alright."

"'*I am on the bridge of my caravel, with my soul tied fast to the rudder.*' '*The Martians have arrived . . .*' He loves me."

"His love for you is part of his plan to take me down. '*Wake up, my darling, wake up: can't you see that the day has dawned?*'"

There is an electric tension between us as we move closer to each other, and she doesn't know whether to back down or to stand up to me, and that's why she starts singing the Mexican national anthem . . .

"He's seducing you to learn the family secrets. He's manipulating you, and he'll throw you out like a used Kleenex . . ."

"You're jealous! *The road to Guanajuato!*"

"Jealous of what? Of you?"

"The ugly guy is more handsome. The ugly guy is more powerful. The ugly guy loves me."

"What about you?"

"'In my delightful jade eyes you can see that I am in love.'"

How can I respond to her?

Can I reveal to her that Góngora tried to murder Don Celestino Holguín? Can I tell her that the idiot failed in the attempt and instead killed a poor pastry salesman who covered the same route as Don Celes?

I don't reveal this because she wouldn't believe me.

I don't reveal this because I know that Don Celes wouldn't allow her to get a divorce.

I don't reveal this because it occurs to me that, having failed once in his attempt to kill Don Celes so he could marry Priscila, the little stinkeroo won't screw up a second time.

And so I must hurry.

The disastrous conclusion of Góngora's plans quickly approaches. I receive the first indication of the plans from my gardener, Xocoyotzín Pereda, whom I find crying inconsolably while he pushes a lawnmower, descending from the heights of my father-in-law's mansion and disappearing into a ravine, which has been strangled by our obliviousness that under our feet the weeds grow and the dead lie . . .

"What's the matter, Don Xocoyotzín?" I say, putting my hand on his shoulder, touching antiquity.

"Nothing, Señor Gorozpe, nothing," he answers with his usual sad expression to which a new melancholy has been added.

"Go on, tell me."

"Little Xocoyotzín," he moans. "Little Xocoyotzín."

"Your grandson?" I ask, knowing who he means.

"It's not true, sir."

"What? You mean your grandson isn't your grandson?"

"No, I mean yes, he was my grandson," he cries. "He was my

grandson."

"Calm down Xocoyotzín. Tell me what happened."

He doesn't stop. He pushes the lawnmower around the vast property, so to hear him, I must follow closely.

He tells me what happened. He was summoned to identify the body of his grandson, little Xocoyotzín Pereda Ramos, on the outskirts of the prison of Aragón. There were about twenty bodies on display for the bereaved to come and collect. Each body had an ID tag tied to the big toe of the left foot.

"The left foot?"

"All of them, Boss. There was my grandson, little Xocoyontzín, wearing nothing but his underpants and with a tag hanging from the big toe of his left foot."

"Didn't they offer you some explanation?"

"Oh sure, they said the boys were guerrillas fighting for a narcotics cartel, caught and killed in Michoacán and now returned to their families here in Mexico City."

"What was your grandson doing in Michoacán?"

"Oh, sir, little Xocoyontzín was never in Michoacán in his entire life . . ."

"So . . . ?"

"He was with me at his little sister's piñata party on the day they said he was in Michoacán."

"So then . . . ?"

"All lies, Señor Gorozpe. They accused my grandson of a crime he didn't commit. He was neither in Michoacán nor was he a guerrilla. He spent all his time in his workshop repairing broken furniture!"

In Colombia there were the cases of so-called "false positives," extrajudicial killings of young men presented as guerrillas with the deadly statistical purpose of proving that law enforcement was efficiently combating the guerrilla insurgency. When they didn't capture guerrillas, the corpses of innocent young men were substituted and presented as "guerrillas"— then they were returned to their families because they were so poor. Who was going to complain? Who was going to sue? Nor was my gardener likely to get his grandson posthumously exonerated.

"All I want is for them to give me back my dead boy."

I don't know if I had some kind of a revelation or if the pieces of the board game simply fell into place so I could see that Góngora needed to justify his position with a body count, even if the bodies belonged to innocent young men. If to this I added—my mind was going supersonic—the punishment meted out to innocent middle class people and the usual suspects—street clowns, streetwalkers, street singers, as well as petty thieves, bums, and beggars—I came to the conclusion that even if Góngora incarcerated terrible people such as the men of San Juan de Aragón and the women of Santa Catita, he did hardly anything to fight crime. Instead he gave the impression that he was fighting crime. By choosing "select" victims, he courted public opinion while leaving intact criminal organizations, their bosses and their . . .

I saw the light. I realized what I had to do to defeat Góngora.

And that something had to be just as perverse as, or more perverse than, any action attributable to Góngora.

Except that I would act in the cause of justice.

36

My brother-in-law Abelardo Holguín would not likely deny me a favor. We'd interrupted the conversation when it had come to the question, "What will become of our soul?" but I'd promised to resume with the answer, "The soul of Mexico . . ."

Abelardo can't shut me out. I don't know whether that is because he always relied on a sole friendship—mine—in his father's hostile house, or because I have followed him each step of the way since he left the family prison of Lomas Virreyes, tried his literary luck and failed, met with Rodrigo Pola, became a soap opera writer, and now . . .

He'd asked to meet at a restaurant, and he spoke to me about the soul. I'd called the television network and they'd told me, "He doesn't work here anymore."

I'd had the excellent idea of giving him the latest Palm Pre when he left home so that I wouldn't lose touch with the only lucid member of that family of dunces. The Palm Pre is a next-generation smartphone created by some three thousand top-notch engineers. It is the most advanced model in the world. The advantage for me is that it still hasn't arrived in Mexico, which gives me a secret ability to communicate without official or unofficial interference. It encrypts all communications. I'd chosen to give one of my Palm Pres to Abelardo without worrying about the consequences.

"I'm calling you to arrange a meeting," I say to him over his rare Palm Pre. "We need to talk, you and I."

"You and I and she," he clarifies.

"And she," I agree, though I have no patience for any mysteries other than my own. "Where?"

"The Chapultepec Park Zoo."

I haven't been to the zoo since I was a kid, even though I drive past it every day on my commute from the house in Virreyes to the office on Reforma Avenue, passing far enough away that those deep and concentrated animal smells don't reach me the way they do now when I walk into the jungle vegetation.

I had forgotten the pungent smell of the metropolitan zoo. This mother of all smells comes from the combination of all the animals that live there side by side but separated from each other and from the public by gates, bars, and pits, insurmountable borders. I am well aware that there are animals that attack other animals by instinct as well as by necessity. With notable exceptions, the big ones eat the smaller ones. And the big ones—gorillas, bears, lions, tigers—coexist. But they would attack us, not because we are small, but because we are different, we are bipeds, allegedly rational, and able in any case to talk. If they could see us.

Because, more than anything, we are onlookers. We come to the zoo, and we stare at them. We toss some of them peanuts. We make faces at others. We imitate their roars. We joyfully scratch ourselves: seeing monkey/doing monkey. We flap our arms as if they were the wings of a bird, and we realize that we alone stare at the birds and the beasts. They don't look at each other. They never look at us. We are of no great concern to them. And we are their jailers. The tiger moves nimbly. He makes the air tremble. He paces his cell as though no one alive could block his way.

The two of them wait for me in front of the tigers' big cage.

I recognize Abelardo.

But not the woman who accompanies him.

She stands with her back to me, absorbed in contemplating the tiger. Abelardo extends his hand to me. Even when the woman turns around to look at me, I can't see her. A thick veil conceals her face. The impenetrable veil reveals nothing. Her voice has to penetrate a curtain to tell me her name and, in the provincial manner, assure me of her gracefulness.

"Sagrario Guadalupe, at your service."

Sagrario Guadalupe or Guadalupe Sagrario? What is the reason for the widespread custom of giving the last name first and the first name last, mimicking the alphabetical order of the phone book?

Sagrario Guadalupe. Guadalupe Sagrario.

She is dressed in black. Not just the veil. She's wearing a monk's, or I suppose a nun's, well, actually a monk's robe, black stockings, and black flats. Her gloveless hands alone give her away. They are the hands of an old woman. Bony hands, protruding blue veins, arthritic fingers that take my hand for just a second, as though she fears that with a touch everything about her would be revealed.

We gaze at the animals. There are more than three thousand of them in the Chapultepec Zoo. A city unto itself.

37

LAST EDITION NEWS BULLETIN

The public debate over the comet continues. The scientist Vizarrón provides us with facts about the history of the phenomenon going back in the West to the Stagirite Aristotle, whose *Meteorology* is the earliest writing on comets we know of, and who refers to them as "flaming expectations."

We don't know whether Aristotle meant not *expectation* but *hope*, Father Güemes claims, interrupting the scientist and insisting on giving a spiritual connotation to a physical occurrence. The repeated appearances of the comet are signs of a God angry over some frustrations of His divine plan.

"What does the divine plan have to do with anything," the man of science responds. "A comet is nothing more than an ordinary and physical manifestation of Newton's law of universal gravity."

"How often does a comet appear?" asks the man of God.

"Every seventy-five years."

"The same comet? And isn't that proof of a celestial plan?"

"You said it," concludes the man of science, "a celestial plan, not a divine plan."

"Aren't they the same?" the priest says in a (successful) attempt to have the last word.

Texas state troopers are detaining and robbing migrant workers returning to Mexico with their hard-earned dollars as well as those on their way to deposit their money in bank accounts. Police officers detain the migrants and accuse them of working illegally. If a worker asks to be taken to the police station to prove that a) he has a work permit, or that b) he is returning to Mexico and has no intention of coming back, or c) to tell them to complain to his boss and leave him alone, in all cases, d) the police ignore his excuses, they pretend not to understand or not to speak Spanish, and as a last resort, offer f) "Choose: your money or prison."

"I am not illegal."

"You sure don't look legal."

"All my papers are in order."

"Your looks are a dead giveaway. Pay up or you'll regret it!"

The authorities in the state of Guerrero reported the detention of Austrian tourist Leonardo Kakabsa, or Cacasa, accused of murdering young Sofía Gálvez, a sex worker in the colonial city of Taxco. Said Leonardo had been detained a week earlier, accused of murdering another sex worker from Taxco by the name of Sofía Derbez, AKA the Can. Faced with the facts related to the death of the so-called Can, the judge ruled that to condemn a young and handsome man like Leonardo for killing a prostitute would only give Taxco a bad name and scare off tourism. Set free, the Austrian citizen Kakabsa soon committed the second crime already mentioned. Detained again, he said that once the sex workers in question had rendered their service, they would laugh at him and at his name, making indecent puns. And worst of all, Kakabsa, or Cacasa, said, what motivated his crime was that both prostitutes had called him "The German," even though Leonardo was Austrian. This time, the local magistrate had no choice but to condemn him, regretting the damage that his decision would cause to the Taxcan tourist industry. "What is more important?" asked the magistrate, "to punish a criminal or to promote tourism, Taxco's main source of income?" The answer came from Leonardo or Leonard Kakabsa, or Cacasa, himself, when he said that killing prostitutes had been a habit of his since he was a teenager, impelled by an irrepressible feeling of disgust and a sense of justice. "I have killed and will keep on killing," said the unclassifiable individual when he was handed over to the authorities of his country in keeping with the extradition treaties between Mexico and Austria.

RELATED ARTICLE

When he arrived in Vienna, the said Kakabsa, or Cacasa, asked to be taken to the crypt of the Capuchin Church to kneel before the tomb of Maximilian, the nineteenth-century Habsburg emperor of Mexico, the son of Emperor Franz Karl and the Empress Sophie, descended from a hereditary (and incestuous) line of Spanish and Austrian Habsburgs, Neapolitan Bourbons, and Bavarian Wittelsbachs. Maximilian's tomb neighbors that of L'Aiglon, the duke of Reichstadt and son of Napoleon with Mary Louise of Austria. When asked about his request, Kakabsa, or Cacasa, explained that his actions in Mexico were simply a form of justice, revenge for the execution by firing squad of Maximilian by the Mexican savages.

Viennese authorities, upon examining the individual's file, reopened two cold cases, both crimes against sex workers named Sophie. Investigations reveal that Leonardo's mother was also named Sophie. Leonardo, or Leonard, is now under the observation of the renowned psychiatrists (despite the fact that the public calls them *Wichtigmacher* and *Besserwisser*, the Important One and the Know It All) of Wahringerstrasse prison.

ANOTHER RELATED ARTICLE

An ice cream parlor in LAS HERAS, Buenos Aires, near ANCHORENA—

Tomás Eloy Martínez proposes the Kakabsa, or Cacasa, affair as the subject for a novel. Nicaraguan writer Sergio Ramírez interrupts his habitual sobriety with an unexpected, wide, and joyful smile. Kakabsa is not Cacasa; he's Sacasa. And Ramírez relates that in Nicaragua there lived a compulsive liar crazed by the incest implied by those few family names distributed among so many citizens—why so many Chamorros, Coronels, and Debayles?

It's not kinship, Sergio explains. In Nicaragua last names are what the names of saints are in other Hispanic countries: they attest to one's existence, they are proof of baptism. That's why it is impossible to know if Sacasa was one of the Sacasas or just a compulsive liar and native of El Bluff who first misappropriated a name of the Nicaraguan ruling class to conceal his countless pranks, such as:

Writing fake manuscripts by the poet Rubén Darío and then burning them in public, defying the collective rage of an audience that considers Darío to be Nicaragua's reason for existing: poor country, rich in poetry. He was imprisoned for disrespect and released soon after.

Demanding that Nicaraguan dictators have their buttocks branded with a hot iron—a gothic D—for two reasons: for them, a sign of distinction; for the public, an identifying letter. Somoza gave Sacasa a taste of his own medicine, or rather a dose of indelible Gentian violet: he had his buttocks branded with an *I* for *imbecile*, which Sacasa announced was an *I* for *imperial*. Go figure . . .

He distributed missals to children with pictures from *Playboy* inserted between the pages, eliciting jesting giggles during the otherwise stiff mass. The priests confiscated the missals and guarded them jealously in their frocks. Sacasa boasted of perverting not the children with their healthy curiosities, but the priests with their unhealthy repression. He wanted to be known, Ramírez pointed out, as Sacasa the Liberator.

"So," Tomás Eloy Martínez deduced, "your Sacasa is our Sikasky, a criminal mastermind from Buenos Aires whose MO included the unusual practice of remaining at the scene of the crime, mute and calm, as though he were a simple bystander of the murder that had just been committed and that the police never pinned on him because he never fled. The military dictatorship employed Sikasky as their perfect murderer. The police always accused the crime's victims while Sikasky climbed the ladder of success, which put him in danger of being caught, because his technique was to be the criminal who was present, visible, and therefore not guilty."

"But he got away. I came across him having dinner, not so far from here, in Vicente López."

"Of course he got away. He denounced the criminals of the military regime. And very effectively at that. He gave all the gory details. He sent his bosses to prison."

"And now, Tomás Eloy."

"He gazes with great melancholy from his table in front of Recoleta Cemetery and regrets that none of his victims are there, among oligarchs' tombs built on cows and grain, but they're all in the La Chacarita cemetery . . ."

"La Chacarita, where Carlos Gardel is buried."

"Sikasky can't stand the competition."

"So, tell me, Tomás Eloy, is your Sikasky my Sacasa?"

"Tell me, Sergio, is your Nicaraguan Sacasa the Viennese Kakabsa?"

"Tell me, Tomás Eloy, is the Viennese Kakabsa the Cacasa killer of Mexican whores?"

"Tell me, Sergio, something I've always wanted to ask you. Can a reader take on an identity in literature the way an actor can in movies? That man who says he is Domingo Sarmiento is really the actor Enrique Muriño."

"No, not really, no, Raskolnikov can be Peter Lorre or Pierre Blanchar, but neither Lorre nor Blanchar can be Raskolnikov. They are images. Raskolnikov is word, syllable, name, literature . . ."

"We *imagine* literature and only *see* cinema?"

"No, not exactly, we give any image we like to literature."

"But not to cinema?"

"Only when we turn off the light and close our eyes."

"A dulce-de-leche ice cream."

"In Argentina, we don't say *cajeta*."

"In her madness, remembering both her husband (whom she always believed to be alive) and the Mexican sweet (which nobody had the charity to bring to her), the Empress Carlota cried out, 'Max, *cajeta*.'"

"And what does all of this have to do with *Adam in Eden*, the novel you're reading?"

"Everything and nothing. The associative mysteries of reading."

"A need to postpone endings?"

"There is no ending. There is reading. The reader is the ending."

"The reader recreates or invents the novel?"

"An interesting novel is one that escapes from the writer's hands. Rather . . ."

"Where in the novel are you?"

"In *Adam in Eden*? The part where Adam Gorozpe and his brother-in-law, Abelardo Holguín, are trading boxing trivia."

"What do they say?"

"Let me read it to you.

"'Who established the rules of boxing?'

"'Jack Broughton in approximately 1747, and the marquis of Queensberry in 1867 . . .'

"'Who was the first professional boxer?'

"'An English Jew by the name of Dan Mendoza. That was before boxing gloves caught on.'

"'Who was the first to wear gloves?'

"'The very same Jack Broughton. But it was the English pugilist Jem Mace who popularized gloves.'

"'On the other hand, John L. Sullivan preferred to fight with his bare fists.'

"'Socially speaking, what is boxing good for?'

"'Boxers rise above poverty. From being an ignorant Irishman or a guy out of an Italian-American slum or a black slave . . .'

"'Joe Louis, champion from 1937 to 1949.'

"'He wound up as a doorman, penniless with cauliflower ears.'

"'Can we divert social climbing through crime to boxing?'

"'By way of guerrilla fighters: the Filipino boxing champion of 1923 went by the name Pancho Villa.'

"'1923: the same year that our Mexican Pancho Villa was murdered.'

"'Don't get your hopes up, my dear brother-in-law. When you fight without gloves, don't move your feet.'"

38

L calls me, sounding desperate. I don't understand. My associates look at me—or not, who knows?—from behind their black sunglasses. I rush off to L's apartment. The driver drops me off at Bellinghausen, at London Street near the corner of Insurgentes, my regular watering hole. Nobody suspects. I walk from London Street to Oslo. I mustn't seem to be in a hurry. Nor like a distracted patient. I hope that I'm not recognized, not stopped for a chat.

I arrive at the front door of L's apartment building with my key out, but the door is already open. I climb the stone steps to the second floor, to L's apartment.

The door is wide open.

From the hall I can see the chaos.

Nothing is in its place. Lamps knocked on the floor. Rugs bunched up. Chairs upended. Sofas stained with a cloudy, smelly liquid. Smashed crockery. The TV screen with an additional empty space. The walls scratched and scuffed.

And from the bedroom, helpless sobs, tender, abrupt, and intermittent.

I run to L whom I find in a half-open robe, sitting at the edge of the bed, crying, then calming down in my arms.

"They broke down the door and came in armed with I don't know what weapons, I don't know anything about that, but they were deadly weapons, threatening weapons, I hid in the bathroom trembling, but they didn't want anything from me, just to shout through the door while they wrecked everything in the place, they didn't hurt me, I swear they didn't see me, I swear, they shouted, they said that they were going to hurt you, that the message was for you not to make a fool out of them again, not to go around killing the living, to take care of yourself, because it didn't matter whether your father-in-law lived or died, but whether you lived or died, you scheming dog, that's what they said, not to try to pull a fast one, Adam, not to hit them below the belt, to forget about your father-in-law and worry about yourself, because your turn is next, not your father-in-law's, take care, this is just a warning; we pried open your saintly little asshole, this is just a warning, we'll be back, but next time we won't be so gentle . . ."

I embraced L, and we both understood that, come what may, we would remain together. The distancing of the last few weeks turned out to be a necessary intermission to refresh and strengthen our relationship. Did we owe this favor—having brought us closer together—to Góngora's police brutality? With L pressed against me, I quickly thought: a) Góngora was beside himself because he didn't kill Don Celes and therefore couldn't obtain his beloved Priscila by making her an orphan; b) only without Don Celes's dogmatic Catholicism would Priscila divorce me; c) only divorced from me would she become united with a fate worse than death, married life with the horrendous Adam Góngora; d) the King of Bakery's murder was frustrated by mistaken identity; e) the person responsible for the mistake was the freed criminal known as Big Snake but whose real name was Gustavo Huerta Matthews; f) the maiden name "Matthews" was an added disguise of Big Snake, because his mother was a Oaxacan laundress by the name of Mateos who, when questioned, first denied being Big Snake's mother, and immediately broke out in tears over her son's wickedness, the result of his having left the country for the big city; g) Góngora's henchmen have begun a national and international hunt for the fugitive known as Big Snake, because Góngora swears that nobody betrays him, and a mistake is the same as a betrayal; h) the inmate known as Chachacha, locked up in Santa Catita prison, has denied knowing the whereabouts of her lover Big Snake; i) the above must be true, because the so-called Chachacha was subjected to harsh interrogations and didn't change her tune—I don't know, I don't know, I don't know, and by the way go fuck your mother; j) having exhausted the trail of Big Snake, Góngora turned his attention to (me) Gorozpe; k) as Don Celestino didn't die, putting on hold Gorozpe and Priscila's divorce and Priscila and Góngora's resulting nuptials, k_1) Gorozpe's death will make Priscila a widow, allowing her union with Góngora; l) therefore, Gorozpe must die; m) but first he must suffer; n) how to make Gorozpe suffer?; o) by finding out what he does outside the office; o_1) he returns home, o_2) he eats at restaurants in the Zona Rosa and downtown, o_3) he strolls the streets near Reforma; p) we follow him during those strolls: where does he go?; q) at your orders, Chief: he goes in secret to an apartment located on Oslo near the corner of X; r) who lives there?; s) the person who lives there goes by the name of L, s_1) L what?, s_2) just L; t) your orders are: to go into L's apartment, to destroy, sow disorder, frighten, and mistreat L, that's all; u) make sure that Gorozpe understands this as a time-sensitive message.

"It was just a warning," said L, in my arms.

I was silent.

L insisted: "What kind of warning?"

I said, "A very inopportune warning."

After we'd made love in the rubble, I finally explained: "A double warning. A personal warning. If I don't divorce Priscila, they'll turn her into a widow. Jesus! And you, baby, they'll kill you first so I suffer more. Mary and Joseph!"

And that's not all he's up to. Aside from the petty details of domestic life, Góngora gets rid of a man whose power threatens him, a man—I, Adam Gorozpe, am that man—in whom he—Góngora—has confided and to whom he has proposed a corrupt power grab. A man who has realized (*I* have realized thanks to the invaluable help of Xocoyotzín the gardener) that Góngora embellishes the statistics of death with the lives of innocent young men whom he orders killed before presenting them as deadly guerrillas. I know—the man whose voice has been addressing readers knows—that Góngora locks up innocent people and sometimes one, or a few, guilty ones, to sway public opinion, in the guise of the guarantor of justice, albeit one who locks up middle-class citizens with mortgage problems and a few millionaires to add a little spice and to quell public outrage.

"He's a genius!" I despair.

"But, baby, you're smarter than he is."

"What do you suggest I do?"

"Listen to me. And don't think I'm speaking as an aggrieved party."

"L, what matters most is, did they see you?"

"No. I hid in the bathroom. They shouted at me."

"Did you shout back at them?"

"Are you crazy? They threatened me. They didn't see me. They don't know your secret."

"And, baby, you're the only one who knows it."

"Nobody else has ever seen you naked?"

"Yes, just a prostitute, a long time ago, and now she's dead."

39

I am led away from the zoo by Abelardo Holguín and the veiled lady who had identified herself: "Sagrario Guadalupe, at your service."

"Where are we going?"

"To my house," says the woman in mourning from head to toe.

"Is it far?" I ask, afraid of showing myself in public given the threats I've described.

"No, it's right over there," murmurs the mysterious lady.

Where they are taking me—and not the identity of the veiled lady—is the mystery.

"Don't worry, Señor Gorozpe, we won't leave the forest or the park."

That seemed true. The couple led me toward a thick grove to a place I recognized as the "forest of the blind."

"Close your eyes," Sagrario Guadalupe all but ordered, blindfolding me.

"Rather, breathe in the scents," Abelardo said more softly.

And yes, with my eyes closed I smelled grass, roses, and Montezuma Cypress, which suddenly became moss and shadow, humidity and age. A metallic-sounding door closed behind us. I moved ahead blindly until Sagrario ordered Abelardo to take off my blindfold.

I opened my eyes in a stone chamber. Everything there was hard, impenetrable, a great secret dungeon in the midst of the center of Mexico City and my emblematic forest. We'd hardly walked at all. We couldn't have been far from the zoo, or from Chapultepec Castle. Yet here the sensation of "forest" and "castle" disappeared as if flattened by some great metal mass. We could only be—this adventurer ventures—inside a secret cave in the middle of the city's busiest park.

Sagrario and even Abelardo supported me by holding my arms, as though I were in danger of falling from some high precipice . . . I shook them off, angered by this excessive precaution. I wasn't the kind of guy who would need their support. I may not have known *where* I was, but I knew *I was somewhere*. Wherever the couple led me, I knew how to remain standing, firm, armored against any surprise. Such a macho guy.

And what a surprise awaited me.

The empty space before me became light, and in its center, elevated on some kind of little altar, appeared the Boy already described to me by L, the ten- or eleven-year-old Boy, with his white robe and his halo of blond curls. A very polite Boy, he said, "Welcome, sir." A frightening Boy. Not just because of his sudden appearance right here, in the bowels of Chapultepec Castle, but because of his perfect symmetry with his public image as photographed by the press and as described by L. In other words, any semblance of "normality" beyond the public pulpit was forbidden in this secret space. Just as L had said, the Boy was luminous, and he was staring at me with authority and with love, as L had also reported, "a powerful love mixed with a great authority." And with a touch, as L had explained, of menace.

I got my bearings and dared to ask him, remembering L, but imposing myself on Sagrario: "Your wings? What happened to your wings?"

The Boy laughed and turned his back to me: he didn't have any wings. Sagrario groaned, then attached the wings to the Boy's back before returning to her place beside Abelardo.

The Boy said, "I don't need them, mom. I'm just a schoolboy, not a god."

"What do you want from me?" I said, jumping ahead of my guards, again imposing myself.

"I don't give orders, sir. I'm just a kid. I go to school. Ask my mom. She knows."

"But publicly you say that you obey an inner order, an order from your heart," I said, remembering L's description.

The Boy removed the wig of blond curls, revealing a thick black head of hair.

"I'm just a schoolboy," he repeated in the darkness below the castle, a space only he illuminated. "I'm not pulling anybody's leg, sir."

"In public you deceive, you pretend to be someone else, a messenger," I blurted out, urgently trying to retain the young messenger. "Whose messenger? Someone's . . . God's?"

"I am both people," he said with great simplicity. "I am a schoolboy. I am also God's messenger to warn . . ."

"What are you warning us about?" I said, trying to control the impatience in my voice. "What?"

"The time is nigh," he said with great sweetness.

"The time for what, kid?"

"The time of the soul."

"What time is that?"

"Now."

"What is the soul?"

"Don't tell him, don't tell him anything!" Sagrario shouted with a fearful voice—afraid of what? Of the Boy telling the truth, telling a lie, or worse, saying something stupid? "Don't say anything!"

The Boy continued unperturbed.

"I do what I have to do."

"Who sent you?" I asked insistently.

"Nobody."

"Why do you do what you do?"

"It's the only thing . . ." the Boy all but sighed, and he disappeared in silence, like wine.

40

As a lawyer and businessman in our globalized era, I am in professional contact not only with governments and companies, but also with security forces and thus their political intrigue. I have business in both Americas, in the Far East, and in both Europes. I say *both Europes* because, for my practical purposes, Eastern and Western Europe have yet to be fully integrated. Consider this: the German Democratic Republic existed from 1945 to 1988 as Moscow's ally and external border; there, along the line that goes from the Baltic Sea to Dresden, began the Soviet Empire and its vanguard—its islet—was Berlin, the Reich's old capital divided into four zones (Russian, British, French, and North American) when the hot war was over, and into just two (East and West) when the conflict chilled. Only in 1988, when Soviet hegemony collapsed, did the two Germanys become unified, although the "unity" took a long time to consolidate. One side, the Western, was already one of Europe's and the world's most important industrial powers. The other, the Eastern, was subject to the backwardness imposed by Moscow's power (the German Democratic Republic was as much a satellite as Bulgaria) and by the anachronism of the industrial politics of another era, perpetuated by the writings of historical materialism, so sacred that they transcended their own time and always applied, as though history didn't exist for them.

The most important fact about this recent history—at least for the purpose of this narrative in which the reader accompanies me—is that many institutions from the communist regimes survived its fall, prolonged themselves in sometimes vegetative ways, sometimes monstrously active though displaced. The latter included intelligence agencies and general repression, made obsolete by democratic laws but perpetuated by authoritarian tradition. Spying and repression were not, of course, invented by the GDR or the USSR. These repressive intelligence agencies dated back to the beginnings of the First Reich and achieved their most punitive forms during the Nazi regime: the Security Service and the Reich Security Head Office (RSHA) absorbed the secret police of the State, the Gestapo, which in the Communist republic was later transformed and disguised by the acronym STASI that, as much as it tried, couldn't house all the Third Reich's organs of espionage, denunciation, and force under an acceptable bureaucratic roof.

I knew this—it was common knowledge—although I never took wrongful advantage of what I knew. Now, faced with the violent situation that I have described here and the challenges (of all kinds) posed by the sinister Adam Góngora, I had no choice but to turn to my German contacts. In Mexico I couldn't count on the police or the army, not only for reasons of plausible deniability but—worse—because of the unreasonableness of their illegal actions.

So I had a fierce troop brought here, so fierce that no legal organization in Germany—now or before—could assimilate or legally justify it. I dare not mention the name of this secret organization, not even its acronym. The reader should know that its members were not—could not be—members of the repressive groups I have mentioned. They didn't need to be. In them dwelled a ferocity that was greater for being contained. Like eagles in the zoo impatient for their cage doors to open so that they might fly and prey, the troops waited until they could once again rape and kill, giving full flight to their eagerness to act against any designated enemy, employing the most terrible weapons and tactics. Their great disguise was the ability to submit to the master, the great lord, the protector of the group's deeds. Yes, they were as beasts reigned in by a shady and disturbing loyalty to the master, to the leader who was superior to them and therefore worthy of their obedience. It goes without saying that in a democratic society of renewable powers, such a *Führer* was impossible. That was the source of the neglect and *désoeuvrement* or unwelcome idleness of these brave super soldiers with enough intelligence to not join the small groups of skinheads and Black Jackets, teenage gangsters who would end up as bakers in their old age, which is, of course, not a reference to my father-in-law.

The strike team—I'll call them the Siegfrieds—preferred to stay in the shadows, on standby, resorting to action only when action was required.

I explained to Berlin and Frankfurt, in communications encrypted by the Palm Pre, that I required such an action.

The Germans agreed to let these violent mastiffs loose every now and then, especially when prolonged times of peace and prosperity deprived them of action, and these days they faced neither internal nor external enemies.

They'd acted, I knew that, at the request of interested parties in Iraq and Palestine, in Pakistan and Malaysia. And so the Siegfrieds were the only force capable of doing serious damage to the Mexican mastiffs of violence: my namesake Góngora, the escaped convict Big Snake, and company.

I said *eagles*. I said *beasts*. I remembered my visit to the Chapultepec Zoo. I should have said *tigers*. I met them at the airport in Toluca, where they made the air tremble. On the highway I saw them run over animals and peasants—leaving nothing alive in their wake. Like tigers, the Siegfrieds acted on pure instinct. Unlike tigers, the Siegfrieds had memory.

41

The reader will notice that everything is coming together, as in a chorus, at the end of my story. Góngora has invaded my private life on two fronts. He seduces Priscila and harasses L. He also undermines my working life. He creates situations in which nothing favors me. His policy of simultaneously attacking and seducing the middle class (by punishing some, which pleases the ones he doesn't punish) extends to the repression of unimportant and anonymous people and to the murder of "false positives" (innocent and poor young men). Góngora acts in order to warn us: "Administrations come and go, but the armed forces are here to stay."

I understand all this, which is why I've brought to the battle a brigade of German Siegfrieds commanded by Zacharias Werner, a Romantic poet who publishes verse to conceal his true vocations of espionage and violence.

I say that *I understand all this*, but I don't understand the small detour I must unexpectedly take from my road on behalf of my brother-in-law Abelardo Holguín. What has happened to this young man, Priscila's brother, Don Celestino's son? How has he gone from being a boy from a good family to a failed poet to a writer of soap operas to . . . ?

I don't know how to define him now that, having introduced me to the Holy-Boy of Insurgentes and Quintana Roo, Abelardo agrees to see me again at that Sanborns on Insurgentes.

I take a seat across from him and wait for the inky coffee that they serve Mexicans, who avoid the watered-down brew that North Americans demand.

I smile at him. I like him. He's nutty. And he surprises me.

"Adam, my bro-in-law, I need to hit you up for some dough."

I put on the expression of a likeable relative who nevertheless demands an explanation. I know all too well that he won't get any dough from his father, the King of Bakery, and I know that he hasn't been able to hold down a job with a steady salary. I remember him in the catacomb of Chapultepec . . . but I don't pass judgment. What does he want with the money?

"Adam, you've seen what's going on."

"What's going on?" I ask.

"Everything, my brother-in-law, is falling apart. There's no harmony. The forces of order only create more disorder. There's no authority. The criminals mock the government. The criminals become, where they can, government. They're like Al Capone, they offer the choice of submission or death. They're taking over the country."

"That's possible. Who knows? What exactly are you proposing?"

Abelardo seems to go into a trance. He looks up at the sky (as if the Sanborns had a sky), and instead of ordering some creamy Swiss enchiladas, he serves up an Aztec enchilada: Mexico is a country in love with failure; all revolutionaries end badly, the counterrevolutionaries only disguise their failure, there is vast deception in all of this, my brother-in-law; sometimes we believe that only revolutionary violence will save us; other times we believe that only the fake counterrevolutionary peace will restore our health; see what happens, we employ violence without revolution, peace without security, democracy with violence. Adam, how do we escape from this vicious circle?

"You tell me."

"On a spiritual level."

"Go on," I say, concealing my skepticism.

"Everything fails," Abelardo insists. "Everything is suspect: the State, the parties, democracy itself. Everything contaminates us, drugs, crime, violence with impunity. What can save us?"

"Okay, what?" I ask.

"The soul."

"How?" I ask.

As before, he talks with a sort of calm, almost religious excitement about the nation's soul, the people's religious spirit, what has always saved us: faith, respect for religion and its symbols and its holy men, women, and children.

"Holy?" I ask him, hiding behind a petty skepticism that doesn't offend Abelardo.

"You've seen him. The Holy-Boy. In a world of disappointment and so many lies, the Holy-Boy, he's someone you can believe in. You know how he brings people together at the intersection of Insurgentes and Quintana Roo? He used to be there every Sunday, and now he's there every evening, and every evening the people come together. My brother-in-law, you've seen how the people he gathers put behind them everything that threatens us?"

The reader should appreciate that I raise an objection: "What guarantee is there that the Holy-Boy can address and solve our country's problems?"

"The Virgin of Guadalupe," Abelardo answers.

To play down the importance he gives to this answer, I remind him of the argument in the press between the atheist scientist Don Juan Antonio Vizarrón and the pious clergyman Don Francisco Güemes.

"That just goes to prove," Abelardo says, "the persistence of the religious subject. Who still talks about the chorus girl María Conesa, the White Kitty? Who remembers the presidential pre-candidacy of General Arnulfo R. Gómez? Let's go back further in time: who remembers when El Rosario, the town in Sinaloa, was founded? When gold was first coined at the mint? When we won the battle of Limonada, huh? That in 1665 the Popocatépetl Volcano erupted, uh-huh? That during the earthquake of July 28, 1957, the Angel of Independence fell? That comets regularly fly across the Mexican sky—a comet in 1965, in 1957, in 1910, in 1852, in . . . ?"

(My attention fades as I remember being stuck inside Zoraida, experiencing every male's greatest fear, castration, even at the moment of greatest pleasure . . .)

"But in almost five hundred years, none of us has ever forgotten the Virgin of Guadalupe, my brother-in-law Adam Gorozpe. She is present in the midst of so much forgetting."

I smile. "But she doesn't exist. It's a superstition."

"She does exist. Look at the street, Adam."

At the intersection of Insurgentes and Quintana Roo, people were gathered for the daily appearance of the Holy-Boy. He arrived punctually, making his way through the respectful crowd. But this time he was not alone. I mean, he brought someone along.

I recognized her by the black habit covering her from head to toe, except for her old-lady hands and sleepy gaze. She lifted the Boy onto the soapbox-pulpit from which he delivers his daily sermons.

The woman climbed up next to him.

"This is my mother," the Boy announced.

The woman removed her dark cape and revealed herself, dark-skinned, brunette, and sweet, covered with a blue cloak of stars, otherwise dressed in white, her hands, her ancient hands, clasped in prayer.

Nobody shouted "it's a miracle, it's a miracle!" because miracles, Sancho, rarely happen, and consequently they have to be certified with lengthy audiences, investigations, and suspicions of fraud before being publicly declared: what you have seen here is *opus sensibile*, which transcends nature because it is an act of God, who chooses to appear in this way, and not the result of popular ignorance, which becomes joyful and amazed when the Boy and his mother appear, but these emotions take a while to surface, as if the crowd at first wavered between the positions of the atheist Vizarrón and the believer Güemes in the daily media debate.

All doubts are dispelled, however, when the ten- or eleven-year-old Boy takes his mother, lifts her up in the air, and keeps her there, over his head, as the crowd stirs, exclaims, and finally shouts:

"It's a miracle, it's a miracle!"

And Abelardo, sitting next to me at the coffee shop, shows his rationalist's and baker's pedigree, when he explains:

"The thing about miracles is that you can't attribute them to nature, but to God, and God is not nature nor is he subject to society's rules. God acts *directly*, you understand, without having to go through natural causes."

"And?" I ask with growing skepticism.

"The cause of the Boy and the Virgin requires not only faith, my brother-in-law, but also money. Dough. Cash. Pesos and cents to spread the word. God, alas, does not provide that."

He looks at me, and I can't deny it, with a certain affection.

"That's why we need you to help us out. My brother-in-law."

42

So many things, reader, are piling up at once that my administrative skills are being put to the test. Sure, I'll give Abelardo a little money so that he can support the Boy and his Mother. But my time and energy are not focused on the show of faith at the intersection of Insurgentes and Quintana Roo.

The Siegfried commandos arrive on flights from Frankfurt to São Paulo to Cancun to Toluca, to throw anyone off their trail. I've prepared everything for them. The guns. The instructions. The uniforms.

They act fast. They act efficiently. Gas masks conceal their faces. The Siegfrieds are almost all tall and blond as their Wagnerian name implies. Those who are almost as short as dwarves, and are called Alberichs, command the troops.

The troops go into battle.

They have a list of Mexican criminals, with their last known addresses, and the names of people in their families, from the elderly to the infants. Including women.

They attack by surprise with overwhelming force.

They kidnap the old.

They steal the children.

They murder the men.

The Siegfrieds leave behind a trail of blood and pain among the families of the major criminals. No one is spared. No one is exempt. The oldest. The youngest. In a couple of weeks, they are all orphaned, widowed, childless.

The campaign is horrible, I have to admit, simply awful.

A child is found one morning hanging from a telephone pole.

An old man is discovered drowned in his backyard swimming pool.

There are stories in the news:

That a woman has been kidnapped—at your service, sir—forever. *Für immer.*

That within two weeks no criminal has escaped being the victim of crime.

That funerals follow each other like a carnival parade of death.

That the cemeteries fill.

That nobody can identify the Siegfrieds.

That the government is responsible.

That the gangs are massacring each other.

That they are out to get revenge.

That they are waging war over territory, money, and drugs.

Now, now is when I tell Abelardo, you can count on the money, count it, but make sure that tonight the Holy-Boy proclaims from his pulpit at the intersection of Insurgentes and Quintana Roo that no, it is not the government, nor are the gangs killing each other, that these are not acts of revenge between men.

"This is heaven's revenge! The angels have descended to Earth brandishing fiery swords of justice! Don't blame anyone! This is the work of God's Providence! Behold God's wrath!"

There is nothing people admire more than an vengeful interventionist God sitting in judgment, indiscriminately laying waste to the families of criminals who only yesterday kidnapped, murdered, and extorted money in exchange for children they had already killed, and who are now dying, murdered, penniless, and helpless against the horrible acts of the Siegfrieds: the death of an entire class. An apocalypse live and in person.

When I see Adam Góngora hanging by his ankles, like a cut of meat, from a telephone pole in front of my house, I believe that I've fulfilled a healthful plan. Let no one doubt: power went to his head.

When I see my wife, Priscila, look out the window of her bedroom and scream in horror (inaudible behind the glass) at seeing Góngora turned into a piñata, I can hardly conceal my satisfaction.

When I see my father-in-law Don Celestino, the King of Bakery, leave the house without even glancing up at Góngora's hanged corpse, I can finally admire the old man's character. Now I know why I've lived under your roof ever since I married your daughter, you old bastard, secret ally, my semblance, but not my brother!

When I sit down in the café and give Abelardo the stipend for the Boy and the Virgin to continue their work, I think of it as money very well spent.

When I look at the street and see the Holy-Boy and the Virgin deceiving my country once again, as has been going on for centuries, I am grateful for the powerful distraction of faith, the millennial deception that brings the majority to its knees at the Basilica of Guadalupe and inspires a minority to hang portraits of the Virgin in their bedrooms and moves a select few to forgive the sins of others.

My associates have put away their dark sunglasses.

And when I return to L's apartment, and L and I undress, nobody but my lover and me knows that I lack a bellybutton.

I am the first man.

43

On the night when my gardener Don Xocoyotzín's walk took him to the Chapultepec Zoo, he approached the eagle's cage and felt pity. The great bird of prey, the rapacious and strong, diurnal, majestic eagle, a harpy eagle of the tropics with feathered talons, fluttered in desperation around the confined space. Don Xocoyotzín, a trustworthy man of the people, took pity on the captive bird, and taking advantage of the night's solitude (when he likes to walk around the city), he drew his machete (the weapon he uses to defend himself during his urban walks) and hacked open the door of the cage. Only then did he see lying there, motionless—perhaps dead—a large serpent.

The eagle, without even thanking the gardener, flew out of his prison, extended his giant, six-foot-seven-and-half-inch wingspan, and flew in search of the open air, the sunny skies, the mountain heights, far from the pesticides, far from hunters and their shotguns, far from the city's smog-filled air . . .

Don Xocoyotzín picked up the serpent and took it home in the hope of nursing it back to health.

He forgot to open the tiger's cage. The animal growled threateningly.

The next day, a comet shot across the sky as it had in the year . . .

CARLOS FUENTES (1928–2012) was Mexico's most celebrated novelist and critic, the author of more than a dozen novels and collections of stories and essays, including *Terra Nostra, Christopher Unborn, Where the Air Is Clear, Distant Relations* and *Vlad* (all available from Dalkey Archive Press). He received numerous honors and awards throughout his lifetime, including the Miguel de Cervantes Prize and the Latin Literary Prize.

E. SHASKAN BUMAS wrote the story collection *The Price of Tea in China,* a finalist for PEN America West Fiction Book of the Year. He teaches at New Jersey City University.

ALEJANDRO BRANGER is a writer and filmmaker. He lives in New York City.